WITCHBOARD

THE OFFICIAL NOVELIZATION

CHRISTIAN FRANCIS

BASED ON THE SCREENPLAY BY
KEVIN TENNEY

echohorror.com

Foreword

I wrote a feature script entitled *Ouija* in a screenwriting class when I was a twenty-something film student at the University of Southern California. It was my first. My professor gave me a B+ for the effort, but I believed it had more potential than that, and managed to get the script into the hands of an aspiring film producer who agreed to finance it. At that point, I left USC four units short of my master's degree to direct my very first feature film, based on the very first feature screenplay I'd ever written. We shot it for a low budget on a tight schedule, and it was a learning experience as much as any class I'd ever taken.

Once finished, the original rough cut of my 1986 debut was more than 150 minutes long. A two and a half hour, low budget horror film with a mostly unknown cast and an unproven first-time director? No chance in Hell that was going to fly. So, I got to work and trimmed the final cut down to 97 minutes. We then sent the finished film out to distributors and eventually received a nationwide release on more than 1,000 screens under the new title of *Witchboard*. It became a box office success and a cult classic, which eventually spawned two sequels and a big-budget reboot, which debuted in theaters everywhere earlier this year.

In the four decades since the film's initial release, the most often asked questions from fans have been "What happened to that rough cut? Does the footage still exist? Is there any way we could read the original screenplay?" My answers to the first two have always been, "It might be on a low quality, fourth generation VHS tape somewhere in the garage," and "I don't know whether or not the actual 35-millimeter film still exists." But now I can confidently respond to the third question, "Read the book."

Several months ago, my agent called to tell me she'd received an offer from a publisher to novelize *Witchboard*. Our attorneys worked out the deal while I began communicating with their chosen author, Christian Francis. He has not only novelized the film, he has novelized the complete screenplay. So, when he sent the first draft of the book for my feedback, I was pleasantly surprised by many scenes I had completely forgotten over the years. At the time, I'd felt I may have overwritten the screenplay, which is why that first cut was so long, but with Christian's deft reintroduction of them into his novel they feel organic, necessary, and in furtherance of the story and its characters.

A screenplay, even an Oscar-winning screenplay, is not to be read like a book. It's merely a blueprint for a film crew to envision the movie the director hopes to commit to celluloid. Seeing my story told in this new medium, interpreted by the author in new ways, has been truly exciting and quite honestly nostalgic. I sincerely hope that each and every one of you enjoys rediscovering this story and these characters through Christian's prose as much as I have.

Kevin Tenney
writer/director of *Witchboard*.

Prologue

August 1955

The waters of Lake Tahoe were so still, it would be easy to mistake them for glass. The start of a seemingly picture-perfect day. But to David Simpson, the stillness felt heavy, as if the very lake itself was holding its breath, already in mourning for what it knew was about to happen.

Shimmering beneath the early morning sun, the undisturbed water rested in the shadow of a tall boathouse, beside which a small dock extended, its old wooden jetty jutting out into the water. Near to the shore, tethered by a rope, a small, weathered boat bobbed gently, creaking as it bumped against the low pilings.

From a hairline split in the boat's fuel line, a thin, oily sheen of gasoline crept steadily down the plastic, onto the wood and into the water. Drip by drip, the liquid leaked, spreading out into the lake in a delicate, shimmering trail.

Beyond the nearby trees, faint voices drifted through the air. The sounds of children singing from a nearby scout encampment. Intruding upon the relative solemnity of the dock.

A car engine broke the song's rhythm, and gravel cracked beneath the tires as a dusty, battered 1950 Ford sedan pulled up to the boathouse. As its engine cut off, the passenger doors quickly flew open. Out came a boy, just having turned ten. David Simpson. He practically bound from the car, full of excitement as his expectant eyes stared at the still waters. The sun had not quite climbed high enough in the sky for its rays to illuminate the lake's surface, leaving it dark and foreboding. David's excitement waned as he felt something he did not expect. Uncertainty. Normally, when they would come to the lake, the water sparkled and the whole place was inviting. But this early, it looked shadowed, cold and unfriendly, and for the first time, David felt wary of it.

His father, John Simpson, was a rugged man in his early thirties who looked just as he felt, tired. With a lit cigar jammed in the corner of his mouth, he pulled heavily as he opened the trunk. Fishing gear rattled as he unloaded it onto the ground. The clanging of rods, the rattle of the tackle box. The reassuring sounds of a familiar routine that dragged David away from his dark concerns about the lake.

Shaking it off, David ran back over to his father

with his excitement brimming once more. He grabbed the rods from the ground and nearly tripped over himself in eagerness as he sprinted toward the jetty.

"C'mon, Dad!" he shouted back, eclipsing the distant sound of singing.

"Aye aye, skipper," John drawled with a happy smile. Locking the trunk, he grabbed the tackle box and followed his son.

Getting to the wooden ladder leading down to the jetty, David did not wait and climbed down eagerly, then stepped into the small boat.

"Here," John called from above, handing down the tackle box. "Stow the gear, would ya?"

David reached up and took the box, as the rods juggled in his arms. He clumsily laid them down on the boat's small plank seat.

John got onto the ladder, puffing the last of his cigar, before tossing it carelessly aside into the water.

David traced the cigar's arc with his eye; it's smoke and ashes trailing in its wake like a jet's contrail. Something about the lake was off. But before he could put his finger on it, an eruption of volcanic brightness bloomed from where the cigar had landed.

The furious flames roared, as the leaking gasoline ignited.

A crackling line of fire shot like a bolt across the surface, catching on all that had dripped from the motor, pooling over the waters.

And after it had caught one way, the flames traced across the water, back to their source.

"David! Get out of the boat!" His father, still on the ladder, shouted. He reached out a hand desperately.

In the span of a few seconds, confusion took over David's face. Then shock. Then fear. Each emotion froze him in place as he watched the flames approaching, spreading wider, faster, and without mercy.

"Give me your hand, now!" John desperately bellowed, reaching out as far as he could.

David's small hand rose slowly, reaching up to his father, toward hope. But his father's face showed only abject terror.

The flames were faster than either of them.

As they caught up to the boat, the motor exploded. A wave rippled outward, sending splinters and shards of metal tearing through the air, punching holes in the quietness, as well as into soft, young flesh.

David's body was launched skyward, on fire, as he flailed helplessly, no time for a scream to escape his now lacerated lungs.

John was blown back by the force like a discarded rag doll, crashing down from the ladder and onto the jetty.

For a long, stunned second, as the noise of the explosion subsided, it was replaced only by the sound of burning petroleum and the hiss of the debris as it landed in the cold water. The singing that could be heard through the trees had stopped. Alerted by the sound of the accident.

Dazed, John dragged himself to his knees, blinking

through the blood that now dripped from a large gouge on his head. His ears rang painfully as he tried to focus.

The lake ahead of him was a wall of fire and billows of dense black smoke, as the rest of the jetty lay half destroyed.

"David?" He screamed, tears breaking down his face, as he saw the boat drifting in shards, empty. Terrified, he looked across the waters... and bobbing among the flames and splintered remnants was a shape. A shape he could recognize from the t-shirt it wore.

Without thinking, he dove into an unlit part of the water. As his body numbed from the sudden cold, his arms swam in panicked strokes, propelling him toward the dark object. An object surrounded by a crimson halo of blood, spreading outward across the water's surface.

It was David.

John did not stop as he grabbed his son and pulled him back to shore, out of the path of the fire. Getting out of the water, his every movement was frantic. But as he rolled his little boy onto his back, he stopped.

He stared helplessly into what had been David's face mere seconds ago.

Burned, battered, bloodied. One eye had been burst from the explosion, gaping skyward. The other eye, still in one piece, just stared blankly. His mouth was now a pit of bloody and charred gristle where his jaw used to be. The damage was terrifying.

John's voice trembled as he hopelessly shook David's lifeless shoulder.

"Please, David, wake up now," he said, pleading to the universe for a miracle.

Though David was dead, he could still see through his remaining eye, witnessing the final moments of his short existence. His vision blurred more and more, as his father's face looked down on him, agony consuming him. But David felt no pain, only a gentle detachment from everything in the world. Then it all began to fade. The crackling flames, the weeping father, everything went darker.

As if rising from sleep, David soon felt himself drifting upward, away from the dock, away from the grief. Higher and higher, like a feather in an updraft, until below became distant and almost unreal. From where he was, the lake looked beautiful again, peaceful, yet indifferent to the tragedy. The sun had started to shine upon the burning waters, illuminating them beautifully.

From where he was, he could see the group of scouts walking through the woods to see what the noise was.

He could see the boat, little more than a speck of wreckage, now sunk like a funeral pyre.

He could see his father, kneeling on the jetty, hands covering his face, his shoulders heaving uncontrollably.

And he could also see himself. Lying small, silent and lifeless.

Chapter One

February 1985

The pickup truck turned the corner, moving along the quiet residential street until it pulled into the driveway of the Lakewood Apartments, which was a converted Victorian house. One of those stately buildings that had been hastily reconfigured into four over-priced apartments. It sat entirely ordinarily alongside the rest of the similar conversions on this street.

Jim Morar stepped down from the cab of the pickup. In his mid-twenties he looked older thanks to his sun-hardened features and workman's clothes. He circled to the passenger side and opened the door for his girlfriend, Linda Brewster. She emerged smiling, with big, round, soulful eyes, and long hair that caught sunlight in its golden strands. She was angelic... at least to him.

"That's disgusting," Linda said, laughing at his joke, her voice tinged with affectionate reproach. "And I mean more yuck than ha-ha!"

"Yeah... but you're still laughing," Jim countered.

They walked to the back of the truck, and he lowered the tailgate. There sat five shopping bags full of party goods: liquor, paper cups, potato chips, soft drinks. All the necessities.

"Come on, then," she pressed playfully. "Give me a clean one. An honest to goodness family friendly joke."

"Clean ones aren't funny," he replied, handing her two grocery bags to carry.

"Jim, babe," she said, peering at him with a mock-serious expression. "Just because a joke is clean, doesn't make it unfunny. Just look at Bob Hope!"

"Exactly! My point is proven," he laughed. "He's no Carlin."

"Oh, Jim," she said, shaking her head.

He considered his words, shrugged, then nodded, thinking. "Okay, okay. What's the difference between a woman in a shower and a woman in church?"

"Oh God, no..."

"A woman in church has hope in her soul."

Linda grimaced. "That's *not* clean!"

"The guys at the site thought so."

"They *would*," she said. "They have the minds of sewer rats!"

"And she was in the shower with soap, how much cleaner can you get?"

As they got to the door of the house, she fished her

keys out of her trouser pocket. "I think I'll just play hostess," she said, "and let you tell the jokes. That way I can't be blamed for them."

A huge, vicious looking dog slammed into Jim, sending him staggering back as Linda shrieked, before laughing loudly. A golden retriever, exuberant and slobbering, danced around them, tail wagging like a metronome on uppers.

"Whoa! Where'd you come from?" Jim laughed, trying yet failing to evade the enthusiastic licking now being aimed at his face.

A lanky eighteen-year-old, Chris, burst around the corner, leash dangling uselessly from his hand, embarrassment flushing his cheeks. "Fido! C'mere, boy! C'mon!"

The dog stopped licking and turned to its owner, just as excitedly as he arrived. He bounded back obediently, panting joyfully. Chris offered an apologetic smile. "Sorry about that, he just loves people a bit too much."

Smiling, Jim watched as the dog and owner walked off down the street.

"Fido? Really?" Linda giggled.

Jim shrugged. "I guess Spot and Rover were already taken."

They both burst out laughing again.

Through the frosted window of the front door, Jim and Linda were silhouetted through the glass. They stood there laughing, until the muted click of the key echoed throughout the empty lobby, and the door swung inward.

Inside was stale and musty, with an almost choking fragrance of faded wallpaper, old wood polish, and mold.

Just as the door shut behind them, another door from across the lobby opened.

Mrs. Moses emerged from her ground-floor apartment. Small and birdlike at eighty-something, she bustled with as much energy as Fido had, rushing out with a trash bag nearly the same size as she was. Her wiry frame, draped in an overly patterned housecoat, radiated her light-hearted energy. The kind that insisted on greeting every mundane chore like it was a grand adventure.

"Oh! Hello Jim, Linda," she chirped, her voice pitched high. "How are two of my favorite neighbors?"

"Hi, Mrs. Moses," Linda replied loudly, knowing the old woman was slightly hard of hearing, even if Mrs. Moses didn't want to admit it.

The old woman eyed the grocery bags knowingly, a mischievous twinkle in her eyes. "Having a party tonight, huh? Full of dancing and fun?"

"Just a small housewarming," Linda said, smiling apologetically, as if concerned the revelation might somehow alarm this woman, who was also their landlady.

"I better warn the other tenants then," Mrs. Moses smiled.

"Everyone's invited!" Jim said with a smile.

"Oh phooey!" she replied. "Trust me you don't want an old dear like me there. I'll steal the hearts of all your single friends."

"It'll be mostly women," Linda said.

Mrs. Moses gave her a wink. "Even better."

Without waiting for any further comment, Jim nudged Linda gently toward the stairs, sharing a smile with the old woman. Behind them, as they ascended, Mrs. Moses resumed grappling with the large trash bag and taking it out of the house.

Upstairs, the apartment door creaked open as Jim and Linda walked inside. The smell here was different than the rest of the house. There were no odors of mold, age, or neglect. The smell here was fresher, with a scent of cleanliness rather than stagnation.

Jim turned to Linda as they walked through the swinging doors into the kitchen. "What time did you tell everyone to start showing up?"

"Seven-thirty. Why?"

"I wasn't sure I told Lloyd and Mike the right time," he shrugged. "Or even the right house."

They set the bags on the countertop and began unpacking in quiet harmony, placing each item neatly into cupboards and onto the fridge shelves.

Linda eyed the impressive array of alcohol now sitting on the far counter, as a momentary flicker of worry crossed her thoughts. "Those guys aren't gonna get too rowdy, are they?"

Jim shrugged, with one eyebrow raised in mild amusement. "Maybe, maybe not. They *are* construction workers after all."

Linda exhaled dramatically. "Oh boy... I'm gonna regret this, aren't I?"

"Now, now!" Jim interjected, joking. "I let *you* invite Brandon. It's an even trade-off."

"But Brandon's not rowdy," she shot back.

"No..." Jim said, "...but he *is* a huge asshole."

"He is *not*!"

Jim found it all very amusing. "Is too!"

"Is not!"

"Is!"

"Isn't!"

"Is!"

"Isn't!"

Jim moved suddenly, fingers out, tickling across Linda's ribs. It sent her twisting helplessly in laughter. "Is too! Is too! Is too!" he repeated.

They wrestled playfully until their backs found the refrigerator. In a laughing tangle of limbs and smiles, Linda gasped, flushed as she took a moment to compose herself.

"Why do I love you so much?" she said breathlessly, half-teasing, half-genuine wonder.

"Because I make you laugh, even if I don't know any clean jokes."

"Woody Allen makes me laugh," she retorted. "Not like I love him."

"And Bob Hope, remember you find *him* funny too."

"And do you see me running to kiss him?"

Jim moved in closer. "It's because I'm sexier, like the paper towel guy."

"Well, I do love me a good paper towel," Linda smiled. "Come here."

Their lips met, gentle at first, then firm and passionate. Their arms coiled around each other's bodies as they embraced.

Breaking from the kiss, Linda rested her cheek against his shoulder. "God, I love you. And I love this apartment. And I'm gonna love living with you."

Jim abruptly stood straight. He grabbed her by the hand, pulling her into the living room, toward the open bedroom door. "All right! That's it!"

Linda laughed. "No, babe. We don't have time."

"Time is a relative concept," he said, tugging her gently forward.

"It is, huh?" Her voice teased, willingly allowing herself to follow.

They vanished into the bedroom, leaving behind only their voices.

"Yeah, it is," Jim's voice floated, faintly muffled by the walls. "When my relatives come to visit, you'll feel like you're doing time... See, *that* was a clean joke!"

The sounds of their joy filled the apartment, punctuated by the soft squeak of the bedsprings.

Outside, as the afternoon light faded into evening, the sky deepened gradually to an indigo sheet, studded sparsely with specks of stars. The Lakewood Apartments crouched silently beneath, its elegant dilapidation now more pronounced in the evening's half-light.

As the night set in, the peace inside the house was soon shattered by the throbbing beat of music, vibrating from inside Jim and Linda's second-floor apartment. The narrow residential street had been transformed. A few hours ago, it was clear of vehicles, and now the road was lined on both sides. The cars and trucks gleamed beneath the rows of yellow streetlights, as figures drifted from them toward the source of music and laughter. Toward the building with the open bay window spilling the sound of its revelry onto the world outside.

In the apartment, plastic cups and beer bottles were in everyone's hands, their faces merrily flushed with alcohol, the apartment alive with celebration. Snatches of laughter and conversation, with occasional cheers and jeers, broke through the music.

Plastic bowls, overflowing with potato chips and pretzels had been placed on almost every surface around the cramped living room. Greasy fingerprints smudged their edges as people's hands rummaged drunkenly through the snacks.

At the windowsill was a parade of what had been

drunk already. Empty beer bottles stood to attention in a row. Put there by Linda, who wanted to clean up, but didn't want to walk around with a trash bag, knowing the gentle teasing it would elicit from Jim.

A conversation started about midterms, soon segued into what everyone had planned for the weekend, then became any story anyone could think of telling, real or imagined.

At the far end of the room, Brandon Sinclair sat comfortably on the couch, an $800 silk suit draped across his broad shoulders in arrogant disregard for the casual garb of the other guests. His blonde hair and blue eyes lent him a polished look, straight out of a high-end magazine spread.

His arm draped lazily over the back of the couch, as Linda listened with earnest attention to the conversation he was now having with Roger. A pale, thin figure behind thick glasses, who was not at all happy with what was being said to him.

"Well, if you don't believe in God, Brandon," Roger said softly but fervently, "then how do you explain the creation of the universe?"

Brandon smiled, unperturbed. "How do *you* explain the creation of God?"

"He *always* existed," Roger insisted.

Brandon's smile widened. "So has the universe."

"Bullshit!" Roger snapped, flustered by the simple logic.

"Why?" Brandon pressed. "Why is *that* harder to

accept, than an infinite God who has no evidence of existing at all?"

Linda hesitated, adding quietly. "I don't know... but for a lot of people it's faith first."

"You call *that* a reason?" Brandon replied in amusement.

Linda shrugged. "No, I call it an opinion."

Brandon looked around at Jim, who was standing in a corner in silence, cigarette smoldering between his fingers.

"Hey, Jim," Brandon said. "Everyone knows what a compassionate guy you are. What do *you* think of the existence of God?"

Linda tensed, glancing sharply at Jim, who took a long drag, thinking.

Quietly, he answered. "Can't say I've ever met the guy..."

"Come on, Brandon," Roger insisted, "There's no way intelligent life could've evolved so quickly without some kind of divine intervention."

Brandon waved a dismissive hand toward Jim. "You can't really be referring to Jim here as intelligent life. Can you?"

The muscle in Jim's jaw tightened, but he ignored Brandon's dig and turned his attention to Linda. "I'm gonna get another drink." He set his empty beer bottle on the table and turned to leave.

"Like father, like son," Brandon quipped.

Linda watched Jim's shoulders tense up, his back to

them. She held her breath, terrified of what was going to happen next.

But then Jim's shoulders dropped, and without looking back, he walked away from the conversation, pushing through the crowded room to the kitchen. Brandon watched him go, his smirk lingering only for a short moment, as he caught Linda's icy glare.

"Real cute, Brandon," Linda said, her voice barely masking her annoyance. "You just don't know when to quit. Do you?"

The kitchen was a haven of relative quiet. Lloyd and Mike stood by the sink, mixing drinks with the reckless abandon of youth, knowing they would regret their actions the next morning.

Jim entered through the swinging doors, disrupting their conversation mid-stream.

"I bet this is—" Mike stopped, glancing over. "Well, speak of the devil."

Jim held up a tired hand. "Please don't. I've had enough religious discussions for one night. When did you guys get here?"

Lloyd shrugged, handing Mike his lethal cocktail of drink. "We just walked in. Needed to load up first."

"And you left me alone in a room full of Linda's college friends? Nice. Thanks."

"Priorities, dude... Booze first, hellos second," Lloyd said happily. "Now c'mon, what're you drinking?"

"Whatever's handy," Jim mumbled, as he grabbed a half-empty bottle of Jack Daniels and took a long, hard swig.

Mike motioned back toward the living room. "Hey, everybody looks pretty fancy in there. You think maybe we're under-dressed?"

"Nah," Jim replied dryly. "They're all over dressed."

Lloyd snorted. "Speaking of which, who's the frat rat in the fancy suit? The one with the shit-eating-grin? We saw him when we came in."

Jim's lip curled in annoyance. "Brandon Sinclair."

"Sinclair?" Mike's eyes widened slightly as he remembered. "As in Sinclair Vineyards?"

"That's him," Jim nodded. "Linda used to go out with him," he said flatly.

"Oooh... I'm impressed," Lloyd laughed.

"So's he," Jim replied, not caring to hide his irritation.

"Jealous much?" Lloyd teased.

Before Jim could answer, Linda poked her head through the kitchen door.

"Jim? Oh! Hi, Lloyd. Hi, Mike."

They waved back and then all stood in awkward silence. A silence finally broken by Lloyd.

"Well, time for me to get out there and find my soul mate, preferably with major daddy issues and no gag reflex."

Then, as if on cue, both he and Mike slipped past Linda, not wanting to get in the middle of anything.

She waited patiently for Mike's response to trail him out the door into the living room. "Cool. I've never been anyone's lapse in judgement before."

Linda's gaze softened as she saw Jim's annoyance.

"You all right?"

"I *told* you he was an asshole."

"I know, I know," Linda said, conceding. "Are you coming back out?"

"In a minute," Jim said, attempting a reassuring smile toward her and failing. "You go be a beautiful hostess, and I'll come up with some clean jokes, deal?"

"Deal," she smiled. "I love you."

"I know," was all he could manage in reply.

Linda felt a twinge of rejection but disappeared back into the party without a word. Jim took another long swig from the bottle, feeling the alcohol burn down his throat as he swallowed, hoping it might dissolve the unease now resting in his gut.

Much later, as the music died away from the party, it left behind only conversations. The crowd had shrunk to a much smaller cluster of fifteen people gathered in a loose circle around Brandon and Roger. Jim hovered near the back, drunker now, cigarette in hand with one tucked behind his ear, unlit. He stumbled slightly forward, peering through the people.

Roger's voice rose, incredulous, from within the circle. "How can you believe in spirits when you don't believe in God or Satan? That makes no sense whatsoever!"

Brandon's reply was calm and matter of fact. "Because there is evidence of their existence; eyewitness accounts, photographs, recordings... You name it." He gestured theatrically toward a Ouija board in a box on the coffee table. "And not just other people's testimony, I've seen it firsthand. I've even contacted some of them. You may believe you speak to God, but there's no basis in observational fact."

Roger eyed the board skeptically. "So, what? You believe this Wee Jee Board you bought from a toy store lets you speak to dead people?"

"Ouija," Brandon corrected, as he leaned down to rummage through the box. "It's pronounced Oui*ja*, not Wee*Jee*. It comes from the French and German words for yes, 'oui' and 'ja'. And this thing..." He held up a large heart-shaped pointer of polished wood, "is called the planchette. It spells out the spirit's responses."

Lloyd snickered quietly behind Linda's chair. "I don't care what you call it, dude. It's still just a toy, like Monopoly, or checkers, or Clue."

"More like Clue-less," Jim countered.

Brandon sneered. "For your information, 'dude,' the Ouija board has been around since before recorded history. It was in wide use as far back as 540 B.C. It was even called a Witchboard in the Middle Ages, because early Christian's believed witches used it to communicate with demons. Kennard just packaged it up, *thinking* it was a toy. Having no idea of the power they were unleashing."

Jim's voice drifted from behind, drunk, argumentative, and skeptical. "And I suppose if Barbie Dolls had been around that long, you'd be talking to them too, huh?"

Brandon shot him with an annoyed glare. "It beats talking to *you*, Morar."

"That's because I use words with more than one syllable," Jim fired back.

Before it could escalate, Linda clapped her hands together. "Let's see how it works. Brandon? Show us?"

The two men stared at each other for a moment longer, before Brandon turned back to her with a smarmy smile.

"All right. Now, for the best results, the Ouija should be used by only two people, a man and a woman. And it shouldn't be laying on a table. It should sit on our knees so there's as much body contact as possible. Also, the two people should have clean, pure systems. That way, the flow of energy through us to the planchette is as strong as it can be."

Linda frowned with concern. "You mean the spirits *actually* enter us?"

"Not like that. It's perfectly safe. You become a temporary portal for them to speak through, that's all."

"Well, what do you mean by 'clean systems' then?"

"No alcohol, no nicotine, no poison in their bodies. Clean. Like you. Care to give it a try?"

"I'm not sure," she replied. "I don't think it's a good idea."

Voices from the crowd egged her on. "Go on!", "It'll be a laugh!", "Do it!"

Linda looked around at her expectant friends. "All right, all right."

"Good," Brandon said. "I don't smoke either, and I haven't been drinking tonight, so together we should be able to form a clear, strong contact."

Brandon picked up the board and sat on the couch.

Jim leaned into Linda and whispered, "I'll *bet* he wants a clear, strong contact."

Linda gave him a 'behave yourself' look as she walked over and sat beside Brandon.

Turning to face her, he took the Ouija board and balanced it between their knees.

"And one more thing," Brandon said. "Before we start, some things you should know. The spirits are lousy spellers, so you have to read into the answers sometimes. And a lot of them like to lie or get a reaction from the living. So, just to play it safe, I'm gonna try to contact David, the spirit of a little boy who died about thirty years ago."

"You've talked to this kid before?" Roger asked, not believing a word of it.

"Yeah, I have," Brandon replied, not looking away from Linda. "I've contacted him several times. For some reason, he's connected to this board."

"Connected? Why?" she asked.

"I don't really know, but for some reason, every

Ouija Board seems to have its own dominant spirit. Maybe because this board was made the day David died?"

Jim scoffed. "How the hell would you know the day that board was made?"

"Because David told me," Brandon replied calmly.

"Okay, but you said they like to lie, right?" Jim retorted. "How do you know he wasn't?"

Brandon went to reply, to shout at Jim, but Linda reached forward and touched the planchette resting on the board, drawing Brandon's attention.

"Come on, then. Let's give this thing a try." Brandon nodded, smiling once more as he placed his fingers next to hers on the planchette.

"All right, so you have to touch this very lightly," he said. "Not enough to push it, but enough to make a connection."

She positioned her fingers to hover over it, the lightest of touches.

"David, are you here?" Brandon said in a deep, theatrical voice. "Can you hear my voice speaking to you?"

The planchette began to move in a circular pattern across the board.

The onlookers murmured amongst themselves, half in disbelief, half amused that anyone would believe such a display.

Linda gasped as the planchette moved under their touch. She looked at Brandon with wonder. "Can I talk to him? To David?"

Brandon nodded, enjoying this moment with her.

"Is that you, David?" she asked aloud, staring down at the board.

The planchette slid across the board and pointed to *YES*.

She could not contain her joyful grin.

"My God," she said to herself, before speaking once more to him. "How old are you?" The planchette moved to 7.

Brandon's expression turned to concern. "Thank you very much. Goodbye." He abruptly removed his fingers from the planchette, severing the connection.

"What? Why?" Linda asked, puzzled.

"That wasn't David."

"Then who was it?"

"I don't know," he replied, looking annoyed at the board. "I told you that they like to lie sometimes."

"How do you know it wasn't your ghost messing around?" Roger asked from the other couch.

"Because David was ten when he died, not seven," Brandon said. "Besides, we have a special signal that no other spirit knows."

"Wow," Linda whispered. "This is kind of spooky."

"This is kind of *stupid*," Jim grumbled at the back.

Lloyd nodded his agreement, "This is a LOT stupid."

"Let's try again," Brandon said, ignoring the disruption.

Both put their fingers back on the planchette as before.

"David, can you hear me? Would you like to talk to us?"

The planchette trembled slightly under their light touch.

"David? Is that you?"

The planchette began to trace a figure eight over and over on the board.

Brandon smiled.

"A figure eight?" Linda asked.

"Yup," he nodded. "That's David's signal. If you want to talk to him, go ahead."

Linda looked at Brandon, then down to the board, not able to fully believe what she was witnessing.

"Uh, hello, David?" she said, but her words fell away.

She looked up at Brandon and whispered. "I don't know what to say..."

"Ask him about Heaven and Hell!" Roger shouted out, his excitement rising.

"They won't talk about that," Brandon dismissed.

The planchette quickly moved, tracing over three letters in a new loop.

B.

A.

D.

B.

A.

D.

B.

A.

D.

Linda frowned. "Bad? What's bad, David?"

The planchette began to trace new letters in response.

T.

O.

W.

B.

A.

K.

O.

T.

O.

W.

B.

A.

K.

O.

"Towbako?" Linda muttered before realizing. "Oh, tobacco!

She and Brandon looked at each other, then toward Jim, the only person smoking at the party.

Jim squirmed under the scrutiny for a moment but then shrugged and took a long drag.

"David," Linda said, "why is tobacco bad?"

As the letters were touched upon, Linda spelled them out.

F.

I.

R.

E.

"Fire? You died in a fire?" The planchette answered.

B.

O.

A.

T.

"A boat on fire?"

A pause, before the planchette slowly moved over to *YES.*

Linda thought for a second before continuing her questions. "Was it caused by someone smoking?"

YES.

This time, the entire party turned to stare at Jim. He regarded his burning cigarette for a moment and then took a long drag from it, blowing the smoke out, defiantly.

"David," Brandon said, taking over. "Do you know me?"

YES.

"Will you return to the living some day?"

YES.

Linda looked up surprised at Brandon.

"Reincarnation?" she asked quietly.

"It's what all of them say," he replied. He addressed the board again. "David, will you be able to choose your parents when you return?"

YES.

"Ah that's all bullshit," Jim moaned.

"Why, Jim?" Brandon groaned. "You can't believe you were stupid enough to pick your parents?"

Jim shrugged, not taking the bait. "At least I don't talk to cardboard."

The planchette picked up speed, as it resumed a more erratic figure-eight pattern across the board.

Linda looked startled.

"Careful, Jim," Brandon warned. "You're upsetting David."

Taking another drag, Jim chuckled defiantly. "What's he gonna do? Haunt me?" The planchette moved in more twitchy rotations.

"David are you alright?" Brandon asked.

"Of course he's all right," Jim said sarcastically. "He's just a *little* bit dead, that's all."

The planchette whipped back and forth.

"Shut up, Jim!" Brandon seethed, before turning back to the board, forcing a calm in his voice when he talked.

"David, *are you alright?*"

Linda looked slightly worried. "God, Brandon, this thing is really racing!"

"Maybe he's late for his flight back to Limbo," Jim laughed.

Then... the planchette jolted and stopped.

No one moved.

Linda, afraid to withdraw her fingers, looked at Brandon for any guidance.

Everyone in the room stared at the planchette. It felt like they were all in a vacuum as they waited.

Lloyd turned to Jim, who exhaled a long cloud of smoke, totally unconvinced and unworried.

"You believe any of this?" Lloyd asked quietly.

Jim wrinkled his nose and rolled his eyes.

The silence held for a while longer, until...

...From under their fingers, the planchette and the whole Ouija board leapt upward, spinning into the air, flipping from an invisible force as—

BANG!

A sharp noise echoed from outside the bay window.

Screams and gasps ran through the room as the whole party sprang to attention.

"What the heck was that?" Linda said.

As the party started, unsure of what to do, Lloyd ran to the window. "Sounded like a gunshot," he said as he scanned outside for any trace of what could have caused the noise. Then he saw it. "Okay, who owns the silver sports car across the street?"

Brandon paled. "I do. Why?"

"Multiple sadness, dude. One of your tires is blown out."

The party soon spilled outside of the Lakewood Apartments to find Brandon's prized sports car indeed crippled by a flat tire.

Brandon pointed angrily at Jim. "Thanks a lot, Morar!"

Jim stood calm, alcohol dulling his surprise. "What? This is *my* fault now?"

"Those tires were brand new! How do *you* explain it?"

Jim chuckled, gesturing lazily toward the ruined tire. "I suppose your friend Casper did that. Go be a dick to him. I didn't do a thing."

"Oh, no? *You* made him angry!"

"Tell me this, Sherlock..." Jim smirked as he spoke. "Why didn't he flatten *my* tire? Break something of mine, huh?"

Brandon stepped closer with a sneer. "Because *I* was in control of the board! He held *me* responsible!"

"You're crazy." Jim laughed.

"You're drunk!" Brandon retorted.

"You're a dick."

Linda moved between them. "Come on, you guys..."

Brandon stared hatefully at Jim. "If Susan could see you now—" he sneered.

Before anyone could react, Jim rushed forward, grabbed Brandon by the collar, and slammed him violently against the sports car, one fist quickly raised, ready to hit.

"Jim!" Linda called out.

He hesitated as he heard her and quickly checked himself. Immediately, his fury subsided into disgust. He let Brandon go.

Smiling bitterly, he left Brandon shaken and the

crowd uncertain at what line had been crossed to cause this.

Chapter Two

In the bedroom, Jim was halfway undressed, unbothered by the domestic storm brewing in the other room. He unbuckled his belt and let his pants fall to the floor, before kicking them to one side.

From the living room, he could hear Linda saying goodbye to the last of the party guests.

"Have a good night!" she called out, with a forced happy tone, pretending that all was okay, and the party had not been ruined.

As the front door clicked shut, the joviality had left with them. Replaced by a dark silence. Not any kind of peaceful one, but a pissed-off void.

After a few minutes of cleaning up the mess that had been left, Linda soon gave up and stormed into the bedroom, her heels clacking on the wood floor ominously up the hallway.

Jim didn't react to her obvious annoyance. He got into bed and climbed under the covers. Adjusting the pillow behind his head, he settled back, fully expecting to be shouted at.

Linda violently kicked off her shoes, one at a time, sending them across the bedroom like high-heeled missiles. She stared at him, livid.

Jim attempted a smile. An ill-thought-out move on his part.

"Well, thank you *very* much for ruining our party!" she snapped.

"You're welcome," he responded, attempting some levity. "But don't worry... the night's still young." He patted the empty half of the bed beside him.

Linda stared at him with a look of shock. "Are you serious right now? Look at me! Do I look like everything's okay and I will just let this go? I'm furious!"

Jim's expression didn't change. "You know you're beautiful when you're angry."

"This isn't funny!" Her voice cracked with anger. Not enough for her to break down, but enough to show that the scaffolding around her emotional wall was not entirely stable.

He held his hands up, giving in to the situation, not wanting any kind of fight. "Okay, okay. Look... I'm sorry about the party. I am. *Really* sorry." He tried to smile again to defuse the situation. "And I'm sorry about Brandon being a prick. I'm sorry he somehow thought I managed to blow his tire out. I'm sorry about stock market crashes. I'm sorry about the crises in the Middle East—"

Her dress landed square on his chest. She had

peeled it off with one hand and hurled it with the other, fast and hard, like a reflex. It landed across the sheet, half-draped over his knee.

"Come on, babe. You *knew* you were taking a chance when you invited him," Jim said, ensuring his voice was on the level and without any tinge of confrontation. "I know your heart was in the right place, but it just didn't work out."

Linda's jaw clenched. She didn't have the words.

He continued. "You knew deep down that it would not go without a hitch. Never has before, has it?"

Her reply was quiet. "I guess, but you *promised* not to start anything."

"And I *kept* my promise," he said, sitting up on the pillow. "You know as well as I do... *he* started it... In *our* house, where *he* was a guest. What'd you want me to do, sit there and take all that shit from him?"

She moved over to the edge of the dresser. Her reflection in the mirror stared back at her. As she caught her gaze, she knew her reaction would not help the situation. Anger and frustration would only make it worse.

"No," she admitted, looking back to him. "I guess you're right."

Jim's urge to complain more about Brandon, about how much he hated him, about how he wanted Linda to tell him to leave them alone forever, was almost unmanageable... but he pushed it all down. Deep down. Keeping it locked away for another day.

"I really am sorry, babe," he said, offering another small smile.

"I know," she replied, sitting on the edge of the bed. "So am I."

The atmosphere settled slightly. It didn't become warm, but it certainly started to thaw.

"I just can't help it," he sighed. "When he starts pushing my buttons... when he starts speaking to me like that... I just want to punch... and maim... and write bad checks."

It wasn't the words that made her laugh. It was the way he said it. Dry. Resigned. Honest. Stupid.

The laugh snuck out of her mouth against all her will.

Damn you Jim, she thought. *How dare you be funny.*

Jim patted the bed again.

This time, she didn't bother to fight.

She slid her bra strap down one shoulder, then the other, before removing it, and crawling into bed.

Their mouths found each other halfway.

A kiss that started slow, not tentative, but very tender. They didn't say any more.

The night crawled on, and the darkness slumbered around.

In the bedroom, behind the cracked door, Jim and Linda were fast asleep. Breathing together in rhythm. Their sweat covered skins now cooled.

In the kitchen, the fridge let out its low hum. But otherwise, the apartment was quiet.

It was still in a state of disarray after the party. Linda had given up cleaning nearly as soon as she started.

Half-eaten plates of nachos lay discarded on the arm of a couch, with a smear of salsa clinging to the nearby cushion. Every countertop available was covered in remnants of food as well as empty and half-full glasses. A few wet pools, where drinks had been spilled, still lay on the floorboards. Pools that were now congealing into a sticky mess. A single ashtray sat on the far counter, filled by Jim's incessant, nervous chain-smoking. The whole apartment stank of snacks, cigarettes and booze, but with the bay windows left open all night, by morning that stench would be gone.

And there on the coffee table, with its planchette resting on its top, was the Ouija board.

That was why Linda had stopped cleaning before going to shout at Jim. She had flitted around like a bee, intent on getting their apartment back to normal before bed. But with her arms full of beer bottles, she had seen the Ouija board lying there. Like it was waiting for her. She remembered David...

Was that even real? she thought. *Was Brandon playing a game with us? He must have been...*

As she had stared at it, the board seemed less like a novelty and more like something sinister. She had known it was made by a toy company, but still... That was no game. That was not fun. Fascinating, sure... But now, after everyone left, and she stood staring at it, she found the whole experience scary.

Outside the apartment, the wind had picked up. Not a dramatic howl, just a dry breath that pushed the leaves along the road. And as it passed the house, drifting into the open bay window, something light tapped against the glass.

In the living room, the Ouija board remained still.

Above it, the ceiling fan clicked once, as its motor sparked.

In the kitchen, the fridge's hum started to throb. A wave of bassy noise.

In the bathroom, behind the closed door, the light bulb flickered before sinking into darkness again.

Somewhere deep under the floorboards, the building creaked. A slow, long sigh.

None of this meant anything in isolation.

But somehow, together, it added up to something neither Jim nor Linda could have imagined. Something had stirred.

Two days later, as the week restarted, the late-morning sun was unforgiving as it baked the construction site far below.

By midday, the site steamed with heat from the bare concrete and fresh-cut timber that lay in piles around the half-finished houses.

Above, tiny smatterings of white clouds crept by like they were not even supposed to be in the sky. And unlike the night before, there was no breeze. No respite from the heat, which made it all that much more unbearable to work in. There were not even any birds in the nearby trees. It was too hot for them too. A hard heat that even turned breathing into a chore.

An unseasonably boiling day, slap bang in the middle of fall.

Jim trod slowly along the gravel edge of the site, work boots and overalls on, his lunchbox swinging in his hand. Even though he only started work a few hours earlier, sweat had already soaked through his clothes, darkening all of the fabric as if he had been hosed down. He didn't complain, he was too tired for that. And his tiredness was evident in his hang-dog expression.

Lloyd walked out of the garage behind him, stretching and letting out a long yawn that transformed into a grunt of annoyance. He was having a tough time working today too, still suffering from a hangover, which was now into its second day of tormenting him.

They didn't say anything at first, just a mutual nod.

Glancing at the tool belt around his waist, Jim stopped. Turning, he started looking on the ground around them, before checking his tool belt around his waist for a second time.

"What're you doing?" Lloyd asked.

"I can't find my hammer," Jim said, still looking on the ground. Almost half-expecting his tool to suddenly appear where it wasn't before. "Swear it was on my belt a second ago."

Lloyd gave a small sigh. "You're a surgeon without a scalpel. This is a tragic day for all laborers the world over."

Jim didn't respond, he just checked his belt again, then back to the ground he had just walked. "Maybe I left it at home?" he mused quietly.

The air then split in two.

Jim jolted back as something sailed past his head at speed and embedded itself in the garage wall next to him.

THUNK!

Lloyd stood, laughing with a big, stupid smile on his face. "There, you can use mine," he said.

Jim stared, before turning to look at what had just flown by.

There sticking in the wall, a hammer. Not a regular claw hammer, but an axe-hammer. Heavy-duty. A deadly kind of tool with a sharp blade on one side.

"You could've killed me, you ass!" Jim moaned, not finding the humor.

"Yeah, but even if I did," Lloyd shrugged. "Then you could've come back and haunted me and flattened my tires and stuff."

The moment broke, and all trace of annoyance

faded as Jim snorted with an unexpected laugh. The sound came out louder than he would have liked, which started them both laughing loudly.

Grabbing the hammer from the wall, Lloyd walked between the buildings and out to a large stack of wooden beams that were piled unceremoniously at the base of the new house's driveway. He climbed up, balancing on the uneven stack, before flopping to sit down. He opened his lunchbox, pulling out a peanut butter sandwich, a bag of pretzels, and a can of now-warm soda.

Jim sat down beside him and opened his own box. But he didn't pull out his lunch straight away. He sat for a second and looked around, taking in the day.

Above them, on the second level of the house's frame, a second stack of lumber rested on the edge. Heavier pieces, bound together with a fraying rope. A single hammer sat on top of that pile. The same kind of axe hammer that Lloyd had. This one was marked with Jim's initials on the handle: *J.M.*

"Do you believe in ghosts?" Lloyd asked.

"What? No. Of course not," Jim scoffed in reply.

"Then what about that Ouija board?"

"What about it?"

Lloyd shrugged, not really knowing what to think. "The way it flew off their knees."

Jim let out a laugh. "That? Brandon probably kicked it. He always was about as clever as a bag full of doorknobs."

Lloyd chuckled as he cracked open his soda can. He took a long swig of its too-warm contents, which caused his smile to fall immediately. "So..." he said, getting to the question he wanted to ask all morning. "You gonna tell me what's up with you and that guy?"

Jim looked at his lunch and grabbed the candy bar that was hidden beneath the sandwich. "You mean besides the part where I wanted to slap his face off the front of his head?"

Lloyd chuckled. "Yeah. Besides *that*."

The apartment door opened as Linda walked in, struggling with an arm full of college books, and a handful of mail sitting on top.

She rushed across the living room and dropped everything onto the coffee table in a stack. The pile soon lost balance and toppled over, fanning the books and mail across the table.

Before she could pick any of them up again, she noticed the answering machine flashing up at her.

She hit the playback button, and the tape rewound with a mechanical whir. As it did, she grabbed the letters that had come in the mail and started sorting through them. They were mostly junk mail, which she quickly discarded in the small wastepaper basket in the corner of the room.

The tape stopped as the beep sounded.

A woman's voice, professional and very nasal came over the small speakers.

'Miss Brewster, this is Doctor Morton's office call-ing. We have the results of your tests back from the lab. You can call us today until three o'clock...'

Linda peered up from the mail, a look of excitement on her face... Followed by an immediate dread.

She turned toward the mantel.

The clock read 3:32pm.

Her shoulders sagged sadly. That's how her luck always went, she thought. Not in screams or shouts, but with late messages and missed opportunities.

Another beep.

This time, the voice was more familiar.

It was Brandon, sounding too smug and too over-enunciated as usual.

'Hello, Linda? It's Brandon...' Of course it was. *'...I just realized I left my Ouija board at your party. Could you bring it to class on Friday?'*

Linda shook her head as she flicked through the rest of the mail, one letter at a time. *Junk. Junk. TV Guide. Junk.*

'I'm having some friends over next Sunday, and they want to use it. Besides, I want to contact David to see if he's calmed down yet... Well, ummm. See you Friday. Bye!'

The tape clicked off.

Linda threw the rest of the mail into the wastepaper basket and looked around. Thinking of what to do.

Jim was still at work.

She had missed her appointment.

And she could not be bothered to do any homework.

Her gaze moved to the edge of the coffee table, next to the fallen pile of books.

The Ouija board was still where she had tidied it away. In its box, slid under the table.

She stared at it for a long time, until she relented and picked it up.

Sitting down, she had forgotten the fear it had made her feel. Now she was just curious.

She cautiously set the box on the table and lifted off its lid.

The board inside looked just as innocuous as it had two nights ago. With its fake mahogany printed finish, antique design, not to mention the cheap wooden planchette. All were nestled neatly in their shallow molding.

She took out the board and placed it on the table.

Staring at it, sizing it up, she slowly placed her fingers on the planchette in the middle of the board.

"Hello?" she said.

Nothing happened. The planchette didn't move. No tremble. No twitch. Nothing.

Then she remembered. She had to have a clean system. It had to be *on* her.

She sat up straighter, picked up the board and rested it on her knees.

With her hand hovering over the planchette, she swallowed before speaking again.

"Hello? David?" she asked. "Are you there?" She paused.

Nothing. "David?" Nothing.

"It's Linda, from the party on Saturday?" She felt stupid as she spoke. What was she doing? What— The planchette twitched.

Just a fraction, but enough to be felt.

Linda pulled her hand back as if it had given her an electric shock.

She sat for a few seconds, watching the board, gathering her nerve.

Then, like easing into cold water, she slowly placed her hand back on the planchette.

She almost had to hold her breath to summon more nerve to speak.

"David... is that you?"

The planchette started to slide across the board, her fingers barely keeping contact with it. After drifting lazily for a moment, the planchette finally settled on a word that didn't need interpretation.

YES.

Linda smiled slightly, though not exactly joy. More like a child hearing footsteps downstairs on Christmas Eve. Happiness in spite of fear.

"Hi," she said softly. "Do you remember me?" The planchette trembled before circling to *YES* again.

Her smile grew wider, as her resolve hardened, and her worry dissipated.

"I want to ask... Can you really choose who your next parents are?"

YES.

She stopped, taking a breath. "So, you *can* be reincarnated. Do you know why I'm asking you this? Do you know what's happening with me?"

The planchette circled again.

YES.

She hesitated before she eventually asked.

"Do you know things I don't about it?"

YES.

She paused before asking, "The test was positive, wasn't it? Do you know that?"

YES.

The word hit like a punch to the face. She exhaled sharply.

"I knew it..." she whispered. She didn't cry. Didn't gasp. She just sat quietly. Her gaze stayed locked on the board. The planchette tracing its figure-eight pattern under her fingertips.

What the hell am I doing? she thought. *Talking to a dead child about a life inside me?*

But somehow... she still believed it. And that scared her more than anything. Then her thoughts shifted to him. David. A boy who never grew up... And she remembered what Brandon had said.

"So," she softly spoke, "If you have a choice about your parents... For you to come back... Would you—"

The planchette twitched before she could finish her sentence.

It shot to the other side of the board. To *NO.*

"No?" Linda flinched. "Why not? Don't you like me?"

The answer came fast.

YES.

She stared down, voice barely above a murmur.

"Yes, you do, or yes, you don't?"

YES.

"Then why won't you choose me to be your new mother?"

What the heck am I saying? she thought. She had no idea who David was. But for some reason, she still found herself asking this question anyway. Was it because he was so young and died so tragically? Or because she was just desperate for a child? She did not know.

The planchette began to move across the letters. Repeating them over.

J.

I.

M.

J.

I.

M.

J.

I.

M.

Her eyebrows raised in surprise.

"Jim? she asked. "You won't because of Jim?" The answer was immediate.

YES.

She frowned. "You don't like him?"

NO.

"But he's really a nice guy," she said, a little too defensively. "He was just—"

NO.

The planchette then circled back.

NO.

And again.

NO.

NO.

NO.

The board then fell still.

Linda exhaled.

"Boy," she said, under her breath. "This kid likes to hold a grudge."

The planchette drifted again.

YES.

She could not help but let out a small laugh.

"David?"

No reply.

"David?"

Still no reply.

Her smile faltered.

"David... are you still here?"

Silence.

"Hey, where are you?"

Both of her hands still rested lightly on the planchette. But it didn't move. Didn't twitch. Just sat there, a cheap piece of pressed wood, on a cheap board made of thick cardstock. "Where'd you go?"

. . .

And somewhere, many blocks away, in the full, unblinking daylight of a construction site, a single axe-hammer sat balanced on top of a stack of tied lumber.

Below, Jim held his sandwich but didn't eat it. He tore a piece of crust off and threw it into the lunchbox, along with the rest of it. Instead, he took out a cigarette from his overall pocket and lit it.

He was in mid-conversation with Lloyd, talking about Brandon.

"It was all because of me getting with Linda," he said, after taking in a lungful. "At least, that's when our friendship was totally over."

Lloyd shifted to one elbow. "Wait, you and Brandon were *actually* friends? What the hell? When?"

Jim nodded. "Best friends, actually. When we were kids. We were inseparable. Living out of each other's pockets, his mom used to say."

The idea didn't sit well in Lloyd's mind. "You're serious?" He spoke with a frown. "How the hell?"

"Yeah. I practically lived at his house. My folks were both drunks. So, I didn't spend a lot of time at home. Not that they would notice when I was gone."

Lloyd whistled low. "Damn, man."

Jim shrugged like it was trivia, not like it held any trauma for him.

"After my last girlfriend, we stopped talking... then I met Linda. I had no idea she knew Brandon, or that she was even on the same course as him. When she and I started dating, the silence between me and Brandon... well, it turned a bit nasty."

"Does he still like Linda?"

Jim shrugged.

"Maybe. Who knows. That was a lifetime ago. I was studying pre-med back then."

"Pre-med? *You?*"

Jim nodded. "Never realized I was such a multifaceted guy, huh?"

Lloyd laughed, impressed. "What the hell are you doing *here*, man?"

"Loafing," Jim replied, looking at his watch. "Come on. Lunch time's over. Back to the grindstone."

Lloyd lay back onto the lumber. Stretching out, he folded his arms behind his head. "Ten more minutes, okay?" he said.

Jim stood up. "Come on, we got shit to finish."

Lloyd didn't move. "Five more minutes, then..."

Jim started walking away. "You're a lazy ass, y'know that?"

"Hell yeah," Lloyd smiled at the sky. "Employment means nothing to me, pal."

Lloyd never saw it fall.

It happened in the space between his thoughts, just after he had closed his eyes.

· · ·

Jim had taken only a few steps away when the sound rang out. Not a creak, not a groan, but a hard, *snapping*. Sharp and from high above.

He turned up in time to see the ropes holding the lumber give way.

They didn't slip; they broke.

The top stack of wooden beams, all 8000 pounds of it, shifted forward.

Jim's voice failed to say a thing as his mouth fell open. It all happened too quickly.

The hammer, *his* hammer, slid off the lilting pile and tumbled through the air. It hit the wood pile below and bounced once, skidding across the lumber and under a pallet loaded with sheet rock. Jim did not see it fall.

The weight then came down a few seconds after.

A wall of wood collapsing in a single vertical wave. Dozens of one-foot-wide and eight-foot-long beams of solid wood falling.

"*LLOYD!*" Jim managed to scream, but it did nothing.

The lumber slammed onto the stack below with an almighty weight.

Jim barely had time to jump out of the way before a large beam clipped him across the shoulder, knocking him onto the ground. He landed on his side hard, his elbow colliding with the asphalt. The air squeezed from his body.

The beam covered the fallen hammer, trapping it.

The dust cloud rose instantly and started to smother everything.

But even through the cloud, Jim could see them.

Those legs.

Lloyd's legs.

Just the lower halves, poking out from under the pile, twitching in spastic bursts, one knee jerking, then collapsing again. Spasming like a dying insect.

"*LLOYD!*" he called out again as he scrambled to his feet and reached forward. His hands grabbed at the beams, pulling them off his friend piece by piece. As he grabbed them, splinters jabbed into his palms. But he didn't stop. Even the excessive weight did not deter him.

His mouth was open, and he breathed fast, as he pulled with all his might at the large beams, barely strong enough to move more than one at a time.

As he managed to pull the first few beams off, they started to change in feel. No longer sunbaked wood, they had become sticky with dark patches of blood that already soaked into the wood grain.

The smell then hit him, not just a faint smell of hot copper, but something more rancid.

Jim lifted another beam of wood, then another.

Until finally there was the face, or what used to be a face.

His bones and flesh stood no chance against the immense weight that just collided with him, squashing him into the beams below. Every bone was crushed, every muscle torn. Lloyd's whole body was burst apart. The blood, flesh, organs and tendons, all now broke out through his split skin. His torso was torn on both sides, and all of his entrails were forcibly squeezed out and flattened in the space of a millisecond. His head was just a mass of carnage, with no features remaining to be able to identify that it was even Lloyd anymore.

What was his chin had been smashed into his collarbone. His cheeks were cracked and ripped out onto either side of the gore. His eyes were both like crushed grapes among the remains of his brain that was now flattened out, tangled in his hair and shards of skull.

All was soaked in pools of dark blood that now seeped out from every broken area of Lloyd's corpse.

Jim couldn't move. He'd seen injuries before. On job sites. On the highway. In training. In movies.

This was not an injury. This was a decimation. In a single horrible moment, Lloyd was transformed from a kind and funny man, into a pile of pulverized meat. Meat with intact lower legs that twitched, as if mockingly teasing him that Lloyd was still somehow alive. He was not.

Mercifully, Lloyd didn't open his eyes to see what had happened, before the end came crashing down upon him. He died quickly and without the fear of knowing it.

Jim could only stare as the sounds of the world disappeared around him. No traffic trucks. No sounds of life. Just a pressure that built in his ears and the slow, realization-drenched silence that he had stood in witness of his friend's death.

He took a step backward and sat down hard onto the path behind him. His chest was heaving as he tried to maintain his breathing, but it was getting more and more out of control. He soon started to hyperventilate from the terror.

Chapter Three

Linda was still alone in the living room, sitting on the couch with the Ouija board rested on her knees. Her fingers rested on the smooth wood surface of the planchette.

"David, hello?" she asked. "Where are you?" She looked sad that it had now been ten minutes without any reply.

She lifted her fingers for a second, about to move, but sighed and put them back down. Needing to try once more...

"David?"

The planchette slid fast across the faux mahogany board.

YES.

Her whole body jerked. She gasped as the movement took her by surprise. She swallowed her nerves from this shock and let herself smile at the strangeness of what was happening, but happy that it was all real. That Brandon was not lying.

"Hello..." she said. "I'm glad you came back."

The planchette resumed moving smoother this time.

Less jolting with more fluidity.

R.

I.

N.

G.

It looped through the letters again.

R.

I.

N.

G.

Then it moved to the center of the board and started to move in a figure-eight pattern again, moving like it was idling.

"Ring?" she asked. "What ring?"

It started up again, without pause, hitting the letters one by one.

D.

I.

A.

M.

Linda spoke before the planchette finished its thought. The rest of the word was unnecessary.

"My diamond ring?" she said aloud.

YES.

"You know where it is?"

YES.

She paused as the planchette started to idle again.

"Can you tell me where?"

D.

R.

A.

N.

She frowned. The word made no sense.

The planchette hovered over the *N.*

"Dran?" she echoed.

Her face quickly flooded with a thought. "D'you mean drain?"

YES.

"Like a sink drain?"

YES.

She shifted forward in her seat, now fully hooked.

"Which sink? The kitchen?"

NO.

"The bathroom..."

YES.

"You're sure?"

YES.

It looped back around.

YES.

And again.

YES.

The planchette then slid across the board. Resting on one word.

GOODBYE.

And with that, it stopped moving beneath her fingers.

The board was still once more.

"Thank you, David," she whispered under her breath.

Linda pulled her hands back. Her palms hovered in the air for a second before she lifted the board onto the coffee table and pushed herself off the couch.

She moved quickly to the hall closet, carrying an air of excitement far greater than any fear of what she had just done: spoken to the dead. The dead, who knew too much about her.

The metal toolbox clattered as she yanked it off the shelf and walked through to the bedroom.

Dropping it onto the floor tiles, she crouched by the cabinet under the sink.

She opened the doors and squinted into the confined dark space. It was small and stank of mildew. She reached into the toolbox and brought out a wrench, moved it inside and tried to clasp it onto the old brass pipe. It was too small.

Back into the toolbox, she brought out a second wrench, a much bigger one. She worked quickly, gradually getting impatient as she had to open the wrench more and more until it fit around the pipe's slip nut.

The wrench slid around the pipe with ease.

She braced herself and pulled on the wrench. The nut fought her, having not been unscrewed for years, but after a whining creak, it turned loose.

After a few rotations of the old, oxidized fitting, the

sitting water in the pipe dripped into the cupboard as one end of the u-bend came away.

She twisted it toward her and leaned closer. She peered into the dark hole, trying to see if anything was there. But the pipe's interior vanished into a void. She couldn't see a thing, as she felt a creeping dread about what she was going to do. All because of a dead boy's words.

She stopped, considering the ludicrousness of the situation. Was she really doing all this because of what had just happened? What if this was her doing all of this subconsciously? Telling herself that she was pregnant, that her ring was here? If she was moving the planchette?

She paused before forcing herself to carry on.

Reaching forward, she stuck her fingers into the pipe's hole. They slid inside slowly, hesitantly. As her fingertips reached the bend, a cold sludge met her skin. Her face contorted in disgust, but she didn't let it stop her. She was too invested now. She pressed deeper, straining her reach, and then—

"Ow!" she hissed, yanking her hand back.

She stared at her finger. One of her fake nails had been bent backward.

"Damn it," she muttered, inspecting the damage. "There goes another one."

She quickly moved to her feet and turned to the mirrored cabinet above the sink.

Looking inside, it was a mini war zone. A mess of shared territory. His razor. Her tweezers. A bottle of something expired before the move. Toothpicks. Moisturizer. A chipped razor blade. A crusted bottle of mouthwash. A box of Band-Aids with water damage. All crammed into whatever space there was.

She scanned the collection, moving a can of shaving foam to one side, where she saw it—the spare toothbrush. Blue-handled, unused and kept for emergencies. And after what she was about to do, she would have to buy a new one.

She took it out and dropped back to her knees.

This time, she angled the toothbrush into the u-bend like a probe and started to feel her way around. She let the handle slide deeper into the pipe. The brush's bristles scraped against the inner plastic as she twisted her hand gently, coaxing it in a half-circle. There was a faint resistance from something deep in there.

A sound. A quiet metallic click from inside the pipe's belly. Something among the congealed sludge.

She paused as she heard it, drawing the toothbrush back slowly, watching the shadows part when the brush's head emerged.

A ring, caught by the bristles, came out with it.

It was gunk-covered, but unmistakable.

She smiled in relief and amazement.

Wait, she thought. *Can David see everything? Can ghosts see everything about the living, no matter what? He knew I was pregnant. He knew where my ring was. How?*

She stood and placed the now filthy toothbrush on

the sink, about to run the ring under the faucet to clean it but remembered the u-bend just in time. The last thing she needed was to flood the room.

Without another thought, she pushed the mirror closed.

Startled, she screamed at the sudden presence that appeared in the reflection behind her.

Someone there in the doorway, their reflection caught in the mirror, without any sound of an approach. Silently watching her.

She whirled in fear but soon realized who it was.

Not a ghost, only Jim.

Her hand went to her chest.

"Jesus Christ, Jim," she shouted. "Don't *ever* sneak up on me like that." Her voice was shaking. Then louder, more irritated: "Shit. *Fucking hell, Jim.*"

The words surprised even her. She never swore.

Jim raised his eyebrows, startled.

She inhaled. Collecting herself as her hands smoothed the air toward him, calming nothing but the situation in her mind.

He didn't say a thing.

"What're you doing home anyway?" she asked, yet it came out more defensive than curious. "You should be working."

"I live here, remember?" he replied, noticing the toolbox at her feet. "What are you up to?"

"Oh!" she said, excited again as she held up the grimy ring like a prize. "I found my ring. The one I lost when we moved in. See?"

Jim looked at it. His expression was unreadable. "And it's such a monumental event that you've started swearing?"

"What?"

"Gosh and darn are the strongest words I've ever heard you use. Now its shit and fuck?" He nodded toward the open sink cabinet. "And since when did you become Josephine the Plumber? What made you think to do that?"

"Oh!" She said, as she let out an awkward laugh. "You'll never guess." She turned the ring between her fingers, still amazed that she had found it. "I asked David where my ring was, and... Well, he told me."

"David who?" he asked.

She looked at him, surprised that he didn't remember. "You know. David? The spirit of the little boy from the Ouija board?"

He didn't offer any acknowledgement. He just sighed. Exhausted, with all interest he had now dropped.

"Yeah," he said as he walked away. "I don't wanna hear that shit."

She followed him into the bedroom.

He wasn't angry. Just frustrated. She could see that. His posture was all tension and restraint. Not explosive or exaggerated in the way it would be if he was arguing. Now he seemed closed off and insular.

"What's the matter?" she asked. "And what're you doing home?"

He turned his head but didn't meet her eyes. He

was grappling with the gravity of what he had seen today. Of what he could not ever unsee. The broken and pulped remains of his friend.

"They closed the site early," he replied quietly.

"They had to."

A pause while he gathered the words. Words he didn't want to say out loud.

"There... there was an accident." He spoke slowly and under his breath. He then said the words that pained him to speak aloud. "Lloyd... Lloyd is dead."

She stared into his eyes as her reply came out fast.

"What? How?! What happened?!"

He took a breath. None of it seemed real.

"A load of lumber wasn't secured properly," he explained vaguely. "It fell."

That was it. Nothing detailed. No elaboration. Not that he knew much more.

Her expression collapsed to worry. "God... I'm sorry. I'm so sorry."

She wrapped her arms around him. He didn't resist.

But his eyes stayed open, staring into nothing.

They stood there for a long time, embracing.

Then she whispered, "I've never liked you working construction, Jim."

He didn't respond.

She rested her head against his shoulder.

"It's all too dangerous."

Jim finally closed his eyes. "Everything's dangerous," he replied.

Linda stood in the building's lobby.

The late afternoon light came in through the panels of the front door, glowing across the floor in a smudged rectangular shape.

Everything here seemed off. Abnormal. Too still and too hushed. Normally, here she would be able to hear Mrs. Moses' television blaring too loudly, or cars passing on the street outside, or any of the neighbors, but there was nothing.

Her dress, a gauzy material, colored with a muted pattern of white and blue, fluttered softly in a breeze.

A breeze that did not come from any open door or window. She looked around, confused about where it was coming from.

Something was wrong.

As she peered at the walls, she could tell they were... different. *Rippling?*

Her attention soon turned to the stairwell, which seemed to be resting at an angle—a few degrees slanted to the right. Getting greater the higher they went.

She approached them, looking up at the long, tilted flight. One that seemed to go on for longer than it should. But that was not all, the color from the wood and carpet lining each step had been drained of all normal hue. The usual green and brown pattern faded into a light gray.

Nevertheless, despite this, and without a thought

as to why, she began to climb the stairs, one foot after the other.

What was normally a short distance to the second floor was now a marathon. The staircase went up and up and up. There at the end, far away, sat the door to her apartment. Tiny and seemingly unreachable in the distance.

Yet, she kept climbing without another thought.

Further and further.

Not panicking or scared, she just stared ahead.

Each step took effort, and her legs felt heavier the higher she got.

The door at the top of the stairs grew larger the closer she got. Not just closer, but *bigger*. Much bigger than she remembered it ever being.

Suddenly, her foot hit the final step before she could tell how long she had been pacing up for.

She came to a stop in front of the door.

It looked just as she remembered. The scuffed handle. The little chip in the corner of the frame. But it was the size. It dwarfed her like a skyscraper.

The handle, dozens of feet above her, started to turn.

She hadn't touched it. She couldn't even reach it, but it still turned.

The door creaked open wide, revealing what lay inside.

Light from the window spilled out of the apart-ment and down the stairs behind her.

She waited for a second, still eerily unfazed, before stepping inside.

Across the threshold, as the door had closed behind her, it was now of a normal size. An expected size.

A narrow beam of brilliant sunlight poured in through the bay window, casting long shadows of everything it touched across the floors. But it mainly shone on one thing. The thing that was on the coffee table. The Ouija board sat in the sun's spotlight.

Unmoved. Open. Patient. With the planchette resting square in its center, angled with its point toward her.

Linda hadn't noticed that the surreal breeze from the lobby was there too, brushing through her hair and teasing the hem of her dress. It did not come from the window; it seemed to be swirling of its own accord around the room.

She slowly walked over to the coffee table and stared at the Ouija board. She could feel it. Her fingers itched to use it once more.

She took a seat on the couch.

Leaning forward, she was just about to grab hold of the board and move it to her knees once more. She was ready to speak to David again. Ready to ask all the questions she had thought of since finding her ring.

Ready to— *WHOOSH.*

A blur of violent, fast, motion, as two hands shot up through the very board itself. Not tearing through it, just appearing from within it like out of water. The hands were pale, long and impossibly strong. Masculine, but not from any man she had seen before.

They reached up and locked around her throat. Choking. The grip crushing her neck like a vise.

Her body was pulled forward as the hands yanked her closer. Dragging her toward the table, toward the board, toward *whatever* was within it.

Linda sat up in bed with a guttural yelp.

As the morning shone in through the netted bedroom curtains, her eyes darted around, trying to register everything in the room. In reality.

The nightmare was already slipping, but its lingering effects still clung. She could remember the feel of the cold, strong hands wrapped around her throat.

Jim was already awake by the dresser, halfway into his work overalls.

"Oh, Jim..." she said, as she started to cry from the emotional remnants of her dream.

He didn't hesitate. He walked over to the bed, sat beside her and took her in his arms.

"It's all right," he said quietly. "It was just a bad dream. That's all... a nightmare. It's gone now."

"It seemed... It seemed so real," she whispered, stumbling on her tears.

"They always do, right? But they're gone. Nothing can hurt you."

"No..." She pulled back enough to meet his eyes. "They've never felt *that* real."

Jim held her again until the tension began to crawl out of her limbs, and her breathing slowed.

"It's okay. You're okay." he said.

She nodded, realizing that it was only a dream, and nothing more. "Thank you."

"That's what I'm here for."

She gave a small smile. "I love you."

He didn't say the words back. Instead, he stood off the bed, kissed her on the forehead, and walked over to the sideboard, grabbing his wallet and keys.

"You try to go back to sleep, okay?" he said. "I gotta get to work."

Linda sat up, watching him with a disappointed and hurt expression.

"Jim," she said.

He paused at the doorway as he glanced back.

"...I said I *love* you."

She said it like it was an attack, demanding his reply.

He stared back, just long enough for her hope to build before it would inevitably falter.

"I'll see you tonight," he said before walking out.

The second he left the room, the sadness settled in.

She stayed sitting up until she heard the front door open. Then, she crumpled backward, turning onto her stomach and burying her face into the pillow. She started to sob, her shoulders shaking, and the pillow caught the sounds, muffing them.

By the open front door, Jim could hear Linda's faint sobs. Quietly, he left, closing the door behind him.

In the living room, the Ouija board sat on the coffee table, exactly where it had been left, and in the bedroom, Linda's crying began to slow. Not because she'd found some peace or exhaustion, but because she felt something. A feeling had crept over her. A sense that someone else was here, in the room.

It came on gradually. Her spine stiffened as the hair on her arms stood up.

Still face down in the pillow, she didn't want to move. It was probably just Jim, back after forgetting something.

She hadn't heard any sounds. Not a footstep, nor a breath. But she felt that something was there, behind her in the middle of the room.

When no noise followed, she lifted her head hesitantly and turned to look around her.

The room was as empty as it should be. The glowing sunlight came through the netting and drenched the bedsheets. The closet door was open just as Jim had left it. She could see her own reflection in the mirror across the room.

She let out a relieved breath. Laughing quickly, feeling somewhat embarrassed.

"Jesus, Linda," she said, feeling her fear subside. "Get a grip."

Then came the pain. Sharp, sudden, and low in her belly.

Her hands shot to her stomach. The muscles beneath her skin became tight and started to twitch. Just as the pain started to subside, another wave hit her. Stronger and harder, forcing her body to curl into a ball. It felt like everything inside her was being crushed and torn.

"*Jesus Christ*," she screamed, trying to breathe.

Another spike of agony slammed into her.

She kicked the sheets off. Pushing herself over the side of the bed. Her feet hit the floor, and she staggered toward the bathroom, one hand bracing the wall as she stumbled to keep her balance.

The apartment around her was fast becoming a blur, as her vision faded. The light from all corners of her sight fading in and out in a rhythm.

She barely made it to the toilet.

She dropped in front of the porcelain, just as the wave of nausea hit her in full force. She kicked the door shut behind her as her belly heaved.

Out in the living room, the Ouija board sat.

From the bathroom, Linda could just be heard retching, coughing, and vomiting all the contents of her stomach.

. . .

The tile was cold beneath her as she leaned her forehead against the toilet seat. Her arms trembled from her effort to stay upright. Her stomach constricted intermittently, and each dry heave felt more violent than the last as the remnants of last night's dinner were now long gone.

Her mouth tasted sour from bile.

She braced herself against the wall and slowly leaned back.

Her entire body felt hollowed out, then filled with acid. She was fairly confident she knew what was happening, but she wasn't yet sure if she was happy or worried about it.

Chapter Four

The funeral had already ended, as a small crowd shuffled toward their cars, parked at the edge of the cemetery. Everyone walked in silence. A feeling of sadness had gripped them. It had been only four days since it happened, so none of it yet seemed real.

Jim and Mike remained by the edge of the grave.

They stood there staring with lost expressions at the casket that sat above the deep hole, waiting to be lowered.

On the lid, a small metal plate had been screwed into the wood. His friend's name had been etched into it: Lloyd Salvador. No "beloved." No "he will be missed." Just the name, along with his dates of birth and death.

The headstone offered no more sentiment. No caring words, just the facts etched in block capital letters. Lloyd's family seemed bereft during the ceremony, but their emotion obviously did not extend to written tributes.

Linda stood a few feet away, watching. She didn't stand next to them as she didn't really know Lloyd and felt that they wanted to be alone in their grief.

Mike, with a sniff to hold back the tears, turned to leave. He gave Jim a brief pat on the shoulder before nodding to Linda and walking off.

It took a long time before Jim turned. Maybe longer before he could breathe easily again.

As he looked at her with a weak smile, Linda moved over to his side and gently took his arm. Her hand slipping around his elbow.

There wasn't much either of them could say.

He nodded to her in thanks, but also in resignation to what had happened. Knowing that Lloyd was gone, and that what he witnessed was real, not a terrifying dream.

"I'll make us a nice dinner, okay?" Linda said as she started to guide him away.

"Thank you," he replied meekly.

"Excuse me, Mr. Morar?" said a polite and hushed voice.

The man approaching from the tree line wore a suit that hadn't been in style since the sixties. It was sagging on the shoulders and faded at the elbows. It made this man look tired, even though he wasn't. With a large droopy mustache and a balding pate, he carried with him an air of authority. He was a cop, of that there was no doubt.

He extended his hand to Jim.

"My name is Dewhurst... Lieutenant Dewhurst, Fairfield P.D."

Jim hesitated before shaking it. The detective's grip was firm, too firm, just enough for Jim to wince.

"You're police?" Jim asked.

Dewhurst nodded once in confirmation. "Homicide."

Linda was wary. "I didn't think Fairfield was big enough to have a homicide division."

"I'm it," Dewhurst chuckled uneasily. "I'm also the bomb squad and the truancy department."

Jim stared at him, confused. "So, what can I do for you, Lieutenant?"

"Do you like magic?' Dewhurst asked him.

Jim exchanged a puzzled look with Linda, "Magic?"

"You know," Dewhurst responded, "Card tricks, juggling, making things disappear... magic."

Jim was trying to follow the sharp turn in the conversation. "Never really thought about it."

"I always wanted to be a magician." Dewhurst held up his hands as if to examine them. "But I never had the dexterity."

"Then how do you diffuse bombs?" Linda asked.

"I don't know." Dewhurst responded. "Nobody's ever planted a bomb here." He rapped his knuckles against his forehead, as if knocking on wood for luck.

"What's your name, Miss?"

Linda stammered, "Linda, uh, Linda Brewster."

"And you're a friend of Mr. Morar's?

"We live together," Linda responded, "Why?"

"No reason," Dewhurst smiled, "I just like to know who I'm talking to." He made a note in his pocket flipbook.

Jim furrowed his brow, annoyed. "And I like to know *what* I'm talking about. Is there a point here?"

"Oh, I'm sorry. Didn't I tell you? I'm investigating Mister Salvador's death."

"Why?" Jim asked.

"You ever been to Vegas?" Dewhurst countered.

Jim racked his brain, trying to figure out where this conversation was going. "No. Why?"

Dewhurst lit up like a kid on Christmas morning. "They have these two guys there, Sigmund and Roy, who're without a doubt the best magicians I've ever seen. They do some genuinely amazing things!"

Jim and Linda looked at one another, completely bewildered.

"Y'know," the lieutenant pondered, "The only thing I like better than seeing a truly fantastic trick, is trying to figure out how it was done."

At that moment, Jim realized what was happening. "We're not really talking about magic here, are we, Lieutenant?"

"No," the detective shrugged. "I believe Mr. Salvador was murdered." The word came out of the man's mouth too casually, intentionally. Said so matter-of-factly to see a reaction.

Linda took a shocked breath inward, as she looked wide-eyed at Jim.

He didn't react much, aside from a frown.

"The rope holding the lumber on the balcony was cut," Dewhurst continued, watching Jim closely. "With some kind of hatchet or axe. A single cut."

"You're sure?" Jim asked as he paused. "Cut? For definite?"

Dewhurst nodded. "We haven't found what with yet... but yes, the ropes were definitely cut." He took a step nearer as his voice quietened. "Did he... Mr. Salvador, I mean. Did he have any... enemies? People who may want to harm him?"

"Lloyd? No. None that I know of. He was funny, easy-going. Everyone loved him."

Dewhurst didn't nod this time. "How about you then? Do you have any enemies?"

"Me? No! Why?"

Dewhurst raised his eyebrows. "Well, Mr. Morar, according to your statement, you were standing right next to him when the lumber fell. Even got grazed by a two-by-four."

Linda released a shocked gasp. "Oh my God!"

Dewhurst took note of her genuine surprise, registering her stunned expression. What he couldn't know was that she was already imagining who *her* prime suspect might be. And the thought terrified her.

Dewhurst continued, "Mr. Morar? Anyone?"

Jim shook his head, "No. No one."

"Any other witnesses?" the detective asked.

"Not that I know of."

"And you lost your hatchet that same day?"

Jim's back stiffened defensively. "I lost my *hammer*."

"But it has an axe blade on one side, right? Have you found it yet?"

Jim shook his head in resignation. "No. Not yet."

Dewhurst nodded. "Just vanished into thin air, huh?"

Jim raised his hands for the detective to examine, "Nothing up my sleeve."

Dewhurst smiled, "Touché."

Linda spoke up abruptly, "Our friend isn't even in the ground yet. This can't wait a day?"

Dewhurst took a step back. He couldn't help but admire Linda's loyalty, but he feared it might be misplaced. And that made him worry about her safety. "Well, I guess that's all for now. Sorry to have intruded."

Jim stood silent as Dewhurst nodded goodbye and headed back toward the cars.

Linda moved in closer to Jim, upset.

"You didn't tell me you were with him when it happened," she said.

"Didn't think it mattered. He's still dead."

"Didn't matter? Jim, you could've been killed too."

"But I wasn't, was I?" He looked down at the casket. "It was an accident. That's all. Just a freak accident."

"That cop's not so sure, is he?" she pondered. "...
And neither am I."

The planchette traced a slow, figure-eight silently
across the board, skimming over the letters with its
swaying rhythm.

Linda's fingertips barely rested on the edge of the
planchette. Not guiding it at all, just following its path.
She had to make sure this wasn't in her head, that she
wasn't losing her mind.

The living room was dark except for the lamplight
beside her. The board sat on her knees as she sat on the
couch.

She didn't know how long she'd been sitting there.
Minutes. Hours. But her arms felt heavy. She had been
calling David for what seemed like forever.

It was only as the clock hit 11pm that the
planchette finally started to move.

"David," she asked, her voice just above a whisper.
"Did you cause the accident at the site?"

The planchette moved quickly to one corner of the
board.

NO.

Linda stared at it, not convinced. She rested her
fingers even more lightly on the heart-shaped pointer,
ensuring she wasn't doing this.

"David. I have to ask you again... Did you cause the
accident at the site?"

The planchette moved to NO.

It then circled back again.

NO.

NO.

There was no way she was doing this.

She leaned in closer to the board.

"Are you still mad at Jim, like you were at the party?"

The planchette stopped abruptly.

"Hello?" Linda pressed.

The planchette slid to *GOOD-BYE.*

It said no more.

Linda exhaled slowly through her teeth. Her fingers remained in place as she thought. In the glow of the lamp, the rest of the apartment was in shadows, and almost too quiet.

"David?" she asked again, quieter, looking back down.

No response.

She asked again in a singsong whisper. "David?"

The planchette didn't so much as twitch.

Linda's agitation grew. She felt like someone had hung up on her, and she was waiting for a call-back.

On the nearby sideboard, the phone burst to life, ringing loudly.

She jumped as the sound tore through the silence around her.

It kept on ringing.

She reached across the couch to the sideboard and picked up the receiver.

"Hello?" she said.

Brandon's voice came through immediately, rude and impatient, like he'd been waiting too long.

'*Linda, where the hell were you?*'

"What?" she said, still reeling from the telephone's noise. "What do you mean?"

'*You were supposed to bring my Ouija to class yesterday. Remember? I left you a message.*'

She rubbed the bridge of her nose. "Oh God, Brandon, I'm sorry. It completely slipped my mind. I went to the funeral with Jim."

Brandon's condo was a testament to excess, glass, chrome, and marble laid out in calculated perfection. Floor-to-ceiling windows framed the sterile look the whole place carried, minimalist furniture sat like sculptures, untouched and immaculate. The place felt more like a curated exhibit than a home, a far cry from the lived-in chaos of Jim and Linda's apartment, with its mismatched furniture, threadbare rugs, and walls that echoed with laughter and arguments.

Brandon, on the phone, paused. His tone shifted, embarrassed he hadn't remembered. "Oh. Yeah... of course. His friend Lloyd. I'm so sorry for you... How's he taking it?"

'*He's just sleeping at the moment. It was all a bit too much,*" came Linda's reply.

"Sleeping? That figures."

'*That's not fair, Brandon.*'

"Tell me... did he even so much as cry at the funeral?" He already knew the answer. "He didn't cry at Susan's funeral either."

"That was different," Linda said, trying not to rise to Brandon's callousness. "Susan killed herself. Maybe Jim felt anger at her for leaving him."

Brandon let out a sharp, annoyed grunt on the line. *"I very much doubt that was it."*

"What? why?"

'Because the reason Susan slit her wrists was because of Jim.'

Linda stopped breathing. "What?!" The word came out like a wheeze.

'Face it, Linda,' Brandon said. *'The man has ice in his veins. I've known him since I was seven, and I've never seen him cry once. Not for anybody or anything.'*

She closed her eyes, letting out a long breath. "Well... you can think that. But maybe he's just been hurt too often. By his parents..."

"We've all been hurt..." he replied, but his words trailed off.

Neither of them knew what to say next.

Linda looked down at the Ouija board on her knees. The planchette sat inert.

She hesitated before she changed the subject, but as she did, the anger slipped from her voice.

"Brandon... how often have you contacted David?"

'David?' He sounded puzzled. *"I don't know. Quite a few times. Why?'*

"Have you ever seen him that angry before? When he burst your tires at the party?"

"No... never. Wait... Did we just change subjects when I wasn't looking?"

"Brandon, please. Just listen... I'm worried, okay? I've been using the Ouija, and..."

"Alone?" Brandon asked.

Linda was startled by his tone. Her reply was hesitant. "Yeah. Why?"

"Linda, listen to me..."

CLICK.

The phone line cut to silence.

Linda stared at the receiver. She reached for the phone on the sideboard and jiggled the cradle switch with her finger, pressing it down a couple of times, hoping to re-establish the link.

"Brandon?" she said. "Hello? Hello?" She jiggled it again. Still nothing.

"Hello?" That repeated word didn't come from her mouth, but from the other side of the room.

Jim was there in the doorway, wearing his bathrobe.

"Fucking hell, Jim!!" she snapped. "I've told you about sneaking up on me!"

He laughed, raising his hands. "I'm sorry. I'll start wearing a bell, okay?" He may have appeared to be okay, but his laugh was forced, and the sadness inside him seeped around the edges of every word he spoke.

"No! Just rattle your fucking head once in a while!" Jim's face changed into confusion, then hurt.

"What's eating you?" he asked.

She suddenly looked sad, realizing what she had said. She moved the Ouija board onto the coffee table and slowly sank her face into her hands.

"I don't know..." she whimpered. "I'm losing it, Jim."

He walked over and sat beside her, hugging her with one arm.

"Oh God," she said, fighting back the tears. "What is wrong with me. Why did I say that?

He held her tightly. "It's all right. It's all right."

"No. No... it's *not*..." She pulled back to look into his eyes. "You have gone through hell and I'm making everything about me."

"Shhh, don't worry about me. I'm fine, okay?" he said.

"Now what is it? Tell me."

With everything, there was one thing she had not told Jim. Something she didn't feel was the right time to talk about. But here and now, she *had* to say it. She had no choice anymore. She had kept it a secret for long enough.

"Jim... I'm pregnant."

He stared at her in surprise. Those words were not what he expected at all. Not that he had any idea of what it could have been. His mouth opened, but the words didn't come right away.

"Are you sure? Have you seen a doctor?"

"I've got an appointment Monday afternoon to get the results... but I already know. I've had morning sickness all week, and all this crazy stuff in my head, is this what baby brain is?"

"Well, it's no wonder you're a wreck," Jim smiled. "You're not going crazy. You're just becoming a mom. Granted, it's almost the same thing..."

She laughed nervously. "You're not upset about it?"

"No... of course not, why would I be?" He said the words, but his face didn't support them.

She moved down and rested her head in his lap. He held her around the shoulder.

"I love you," she said.

"I know," came the reply he always defaulted to.

"And you love me, Jim. Even if you can't admit it... *I* know you do."

He stroked her hair.

But his thoughts were somewhere else.

An unmarked police car had sat parked across from the Lakewood Apartments for the last few hours. Inside, Lieutenant Dewhurst peeled and ate an orange from a bag of oranges sitting on his passenger's seat.

He watched out of his open window toward Jim and Linda's apartment. It was only when the lamp in their bay window was switched off, and they had gone to bed, that his work for the night was done.

Checking his watch, he reached for the keys, turned on the ignition, and eased the car away from the curb.

* * *

The sprinkler's rhythmic clicking was the first sound in the neighborhood. It ticked in a lazy half-circle over the patchy lawn in front of the Lakewood Apartments, flinging beads of water across the grass and onto the sidewalks. A hose snaked its way from the spigot, bumping over cracks in the path to an outside faucet sticking out from the side of the house.

As with every Sunday morning, Mrs. Moses stood by the porch, dressed in her housecoat, watering can in hand. She was hunched over, watering her potted plants ceremoniously.

The rumble of an engine caught her attention as Jim's pickup drove into the driveway. Linda climbed out from behind the wheel, holding an armful of textbooks.

"Good morning," Mrs. Moses called over loudly. "My, you certainly are up early on the Lord's Day."

Linda smiled politely, too tired to fake any genuine warmth. "I had to go to the library. I've got a term paper due that I haven't even started."

As she stepped onto the porch, Chris rounded the corner with Fido. The dog strained forward, tongue out as his tail wagged into a blur.

Chris waved. "Good morning!"

"Hi, Chris," Mrs. Moses called out. "How are—"

Fido suddenly lunged. His usual happy demeanor gone as a savage, wet-throated bark shot from its mouth. It pulled violently at the leash, teeth bared in growls. And the aim of its ire was Linda.

She moved back up the porch, afraid, the books clutched against her chest like a shield.

"Fido, stop it! *Stop it!*" Chris yelled as he yanked hard on the leash, trying to restrain the snarling animal.

"For heaven's sake, get him out of here!" Mrs. Moses shouted, moving herself between the dog and Linda. She gestured sharply with her watering can toward the path they had come down.

"I don't understand it," Chris said. "*Stop it*! He's never done this before... I'm so sorry..."

The dog twisted and barked again. Its hackles were up, its eyes locked on Linda, its teeth bared hungrily.

Chris soon managed to drag Fido down the sidewalk, barking until it disappeared around the corner.

Linda stood in silence, unsure of what had happened. As the shock started to wear off, she let out a nervous laugh.

Mrs. Moses laughed too.

"Are you okay, my dear?" the old woman asked. "Fido is usually such a lovely dog."

Linda nodded slowly, still watching the spot where the dog had stood its ground. "Yeah.... I guess... he doesn't like me."

From down the street, they could still both hear Fido barking for blood.

In the apartment, Jim was busy with his toolbox open.

He had the receiver of the phone cradled under his chin, his other hand jiggling the cradle switch.

But there was nothing. No tone. No click. Just dead emptiness.

Linda had told him that the phone had cut off during her call with Brandon and had not worked since. And since Jim didn't want them to pay $50 for a stranger to fix something he probably could, he had taken the work upon himself. Not that he had a clue what the issue was.

He set the phone down and moved the end table out of the way, to where the telephone socket was on the wall. Unplugging the cable, he then grabbed a screwdriver. Removing one screw at a time from the faceplate, until it came away revealing a mass of electronics beneath. A collection of half a dozen small, multi-colored wires that led from the small rectangular socket inside.

He frowned.

"What the hell?" he muttered.

All the wires had been cut. Clean. No wear, no fray, just sliced and no longer connected.

He peered closer for a better look. As he did, the wires suddenly flared with a burst of white light. A hot, electric zap. Jim jerked backward just as the current surged at him. Hitting him in the chest.

He was hurled backward, stunned as the breath was electrocuted out of him. Landing on his back by the coffee table.

Everything went dark in his eyeline for the shortest of seconds.

Then it came back in a blurry haze.

Jim's eyes fluttered as he fought to sit up, and between the pulsing lights in his vision, he could see something, or more specifically, some*one*...

...there...

...standing by the bookshelf next to the now burnt-out socket.

His vision was smeared; colors and details bled into each other. The shapes in his sight were unsteady and quivering. But ahead of him, a figure looked down.

A tall man in his late fifties, wearing a coat that didn't belong in this decade. Or even the last. Looking like he was straight from an old gangster movie. Peering down. Through his white beard, the man smiled. But not a smile of joy. One of cruelty. And to match, his eyes stared wide with hate.

Jim tried to see through the blur, but he could not regain control. He tried to sit up more, but his arms wouldn't move. He felt like he was heavily drugged, unable to stave off the darkness.

His heartbeat was pounding in his ears, almost deafening him.

The hatefully smiling man blurred even more as Jim squeezed his eyelids tight, trying to blink the impossible vision away.

When he opened them again, the man was indeed gone. But in his place was someone else. A woman. Young and blonde. Someone who, even through his blurred vision and his body's weakness, Jim knew who it was.

It was Susan. His ex-girlfriend.

Her arms hung loosely at her sides, as blood poured uncontrollably from large vertical slices along her fore-arms. Slices that traced from her elbow pit to her wrists. Thick widening lines that leaked from her lacerated arteries, down her arms and onto the floor.

Jim couldn't speak. He could only shake his head slowly as he looked up at her. Not believing what was standing in front of him.

She looked down with a kind smile, not cruel like the man who had appeared before. Stepping forward slowly, she moved like she was in some kind of watery dream.

He could only watch helplessly as she knelt beside him, lowering her face toward him to kiss him. The blood still falling in a torrent from out of her open wounds.

She got closer, and he got more terrified.

"I'm sorry," he gasped through his fear. "I'm so sorry."

"Come on, Jim. Come on. Breathe. Please. Breathe."

Linda tilted his unconscious head back as her hands moved over his sternum, pressing down in a rhythmic, panicked beat. Massaging his heart to bring him back.

1.

2.

3.

4.

5.

She quickly took a deep breath, leaned down, and placed her mouth over his, exhaling deeply. Then, taking another breath, she repeated the procedure.

She fought the tears threatening in her eyes, as she moved back to the compressions.

1.

2.

3.

4.

5.

Nothing was happening. Jim lay still.

She moved back over him, looking upward with closed eyes.

"Please, please, please," she prayed to any God that may hear her.

One more round of breaths. She took in as much oxygen as she could, before pressing her mouth to his.

Finally, he moved. A sputtering, involuntary jerk of the lungs as he came to. He moved his head to one side, groggily. His chest heaved as his lungs took in their own breaths.

Linda gasped in relief and fell back, sobbing and laughing all at once. Unsure of what she should be feeling as she ran her fingers through her now sweat matted hair.

He looked to her, his vision strained and still blurry.

"Hi," he said in a weak, confused and cracked voice. "Is it time to get up?"

Linda laughed with relief, wiping tears from her eyes.

He blinked at her, dazed, not understanding what had happened. In his mind, he had just woken and was lying in bed. But as his eyesight came back into focus and the pain throbbed throughout in his body, he felt the solid floor beneath him.

"What happened?" he asked, noticing her tears. "What's the matter?"

She replied through a forced smile. "You electrocuted yourself. Why couldn't you just wait for an electrician?"

Jim slowly rubbed his head. "The phone... I remember." He looked at the charred outlet on the wall. "The wires... I saw they were all cut," he said, sounding very unsure. "I think... I can't... I..." His words fell away.

"Well, whatever you did, you did it wrong, babe."

"No... I never touched anything, didn't even get close. I took off the plate and looked. It just... went off. Burned right up in front of me."

Linda frowned as she saw the screwdriver next to the face plate and small collection of screws. "Babe, are you sure? You obviously did touch—" She stopped talking as she noticed his pained expression. "You weren't breathing, Jim... Thank God you taught me CPR, or you'd still be dead."

"What?" Jim said as he looked at her worried. "But I never even lost consciousness."

"Jim... your heart *stopped*. You were dead! I've been doing CPR for over two minutes.

His face shifted into a deep confusion, but he felt the pain in his chest.

She moved closer and held onto him tightly.

"But you're back," she whispered. "It's all that matters."

He closed his eyes, trying to make sense of it all, before looking back at the wall. But now nothing was as it had been only moments ago. There were no scorch marks from the outlet. The phone wires inside were intact as they should have been. No cut wires. No damage at all. Just a removed faceplate and screws sitting on the floor.

He peered at the floor in front of the bookcase.

There was no blood. No sign of Susan or that strange man.

No sign of anything that he would have sworn he just witnessed.

The alarm buzzed loudly. An ugly electric siren sound.

6:00 a.m., its red digits flashed into the dark bedroom.

Jim's hand emerged from the covers and slapped the large 'off' button on the top.

He rolled over and reached across the bed instinctively, expecting Linda to be there, but there was no one. That side of the bed was empty, cold and untouched. She had not come to bed.

He sat up slowly. The bedroom around him was dim, filled with faint light through the curtains of the morning sun.

The place felt off as he walked barefoot to the kitchen, like it had been rearranged slightly in his sleep. He looked at the side table as he approached the kitchen. It had always been there, he knew that much, but it just seemed different now. But he could not tell what it was that seemed to have changed. He shook off the feeling, chalking it up to electrocution aftereffects.

Linda was there in the kitchen.

Not at the table. Not by the sink. But *on* the counter, legs swinging slightly, robe hanging off one shoulder. In one hand, she held an open ketchup bottle. In the other, a plain hotdog. She dipped the meat directly into the narrow neck of the bottle then took a bite. No bun. No plate. No care.

"What're you doing?" he asked, staring at her as she chewed lazily. "You don't have your first class 'til ten, right?"

She nodded.

"Didn't sleep."

"Another nightmare?" She shrugged.

"Maybe you should mention them to your doctor when you see her."

"Yeah... maybe," she said, dipping the cold sausage into the ketchup again and taking another bite. "I will," she added, chewing.

He walked up next to her, staring at the sausage.

"What are you eating?" he asked. She held up the hot dog.

"Did we run out of buns?"

"No. It's not hot." She stared at it, then took another bite of its pink meat. "I didn't cook it."

Jim grimaced. "What the hell? That can't be good for you."

"Guess this is cravings?" she replied. Not looking too concerned about it.

"No wonder you have nightmares." She smiled.

He took the ketchup bottle from her and set it on the countertop.

"Look," he said gently, "I gotta get to work. And you really should try to get some sleep... Without eating any more uncooked meat!"

Then, without warning, he scooped her up, one arm under knees, one behind her back. Over the threshold style.

"Hey! What's this? I can walk."

"No way. You're a mother now."

"Awwww, my prince," she said, laughing. "Take me to Camelot."

"Can't afford that... Would you settle for an hour's parking in a car lot?"

The door swung shut behind them as he walked down the hallway to the bedroom.

"Ew, don't try to kiss me with your raw meat mouth!" he said. "And yes, I hear the irony now that I've said it out loud."

"Oh, my God, Jim," she laughed. "Don't be crude when you're right in the middle of being so romantic."

Later that morning, the apartment was quiet again.

With Jim at work, Linda was sleeping a dreamless sleep, curled into the pillows with one arm slung across the empty half of the bed. Her breathing was deep and throaty, on the cusp of snoring.

From the living room, a buzz sounded. Not an alarm this time.

It was a sound Linda could just about hear in the darkness of her mind.

It came again.

It buzzed again, longer this time, more persistently.

Outside the building, Brandon stood at the front of the door, one hand pressed to the buzzer.

He released it. Waited. Pressed it again, harder this time.

His car sat idling in the driveway behind him, its door wide open.

He didn't look impressed or happy at all.

Linda stirred, the buzzing starting to drag her back into consciousness.

She turned over. Her eyes fluttered as the sound continued.

It took all her willpower to sit up, let alone get out of bed and pad her way to the intercom box by the door.

It took a few minutes, but eventually she was there, pressing the *talk* button.

"Hello?" she said weakly into the microphone.

There was no response.

Outside, Brandon was already getting back into his car, having given up trying to call.

Linda's voice crackled over the speaker. "Hello? Is anybody there?"

He did not hear her as his car pulled away.

Linda stood by the intercom, still half-asleep. Waiting, before exhaling loudly and pressing the button again.

"Hello?"

Still no answer.

She stumbled back toward the bedroom, wanting to crawl under the covers again.

Then she saw it.

The Ouija board sat open on the coffee table.

The board she had put away. Now there, open and waiting.

She hesitated for a second before giving in and walking over to sit on the couch. If she had thought about it properly, she would have found it all too weird. The only person who could have put out the board is

Jim, and he would not have dared. The only other explanation defied logic and was a surreal prospect. But she was too tired to consider any of that.

She picked up the board and placed it on her lap, moving her fingers gently onto the planchette.

"David?" she said aloud.

Expecting nothing and getting nothing. The planchette beneath her touch was still.

She took a second to think.

"David? I know you're here," she said, not knowing anything in truth. "Stop messing around and talk to me." Her tone sounded almost parental. Something she had not expected.

And to that, the board responded. Slowly, the planchette began to move in its looping, figure-eight pattern.

She exhaled with relief.

"That's better. Now tell me... I have to know, okay? I asked before you vanished, and now he has been hurt, so... tell me are you still angry with Jim?"

The planchette moved to NO.

"Please just say the truth, I won't be angry. Did you try to hurt him? With that phone outlet?"

NO.

She stared as the planchette moved back to a circling figure-eight.

"I wish I could believe you... but I have to say, David... I'm not sure. You burst the tires at the party. My call to Brandon got cut off after I talked about you. Then Jim got hurt trying to fix the phone? So, I'm sorry if you are telling the truth and didn't do it, but I have to return the board to Brandon today."

The planchette shot across the board to *NO*, then began to circle it.

"I'm sorry, David," she said. "I've already made up my mind. I just can't take any chances."

She pulled her hands away, and the planchette stopped in its tracks.

She placed the board back onto the table, stood up and walked toward the kitchen.

The refrigerator opened, and Linda reached inside, pulling out a half-full bottle of orange juice. Reaching for a glass from the cupboard, she began to pour herself a drink.

Stopping, she peered down at the liquid in the glass and started to think about what was actually happening. Was she really talking to a dead boy? Someone who died and is now somehow alive and talking to her through a toy?

Behind her, a metallic clink made her jump, as a butcher's knife launched itself from the rack beside the fridge.

It moved fast. Too fast. Not dropped, or bumped, but thrown.

It landed with a THUNK in the center of the floor.

Linda screamed as she dropped her drink and bottle. Both went smashing to the tiles in a sprawl of glass and orange juice. She staggered back in terror.

The knife stood upright, its pointed blade buried in the floor.

Behind her, something else shifted, making a scraping sound.

The ketchup bottle spun out past her and rose into the air before smashing down.

Its red, thick contents splashed, but as it fell, it did not stay still. It began to move. The thick ketchup undulated as it spread out, crawling into a pattern.

She could not believe what she was witnessing. So terrified that she couldn't even scream. She just stared as the ketchup began to take on a shape.

The liquid spread in front of her, forming a crude outline. A head, two arms, two legs, all in a human form. The blade of the knife stabbed into the floor exactly where the heart should be.

It looked like a police outline of a body, but the murder weapon was still there.

Linda didn't wait any longer. She turned and ran.

She ran into the living room, reached for the front door handle and yanked at it, desperate to escape.

But it was stuck.

She pulled again, harder, rattling the handle in its frame.

The door wasn't locked, but it still wouldn't open.

She moved toward the open bay window, intent on climbing down the trellis outside. But before she could even get halfway across the room, the outside shutters unclipped on their own and slammed shut. Plunging the living room into darkness and cutting off her intended escape.

White with horror, Linda stood in the middle of the room, not knowing what else to do.

Something was here.

Something was behind her.

As she felt something touch her back, Linda's screams pierced through the narrow slats of the bay window shutters.

Chapter Five

The construction site was deafening in a roar of power tools and the thrum of generators. Everything else here added to that noise; hammers, shouted conversations, a radio belting out a rock song through badly tuned static.

The bones of homes that had been erected were frames of wood and half-hung drywall. In all, a skeletal suburbia in progress that had been washed clean of the remnants of Lloyd Salvador. The offending pile of lumber was cleared, washed and repurposed.

Brandon had walked through the maze of construction workers dressed in a finely pressed shirt and slacks. Clothing that didn't belong anywhere near hard labor.

He was now in front of Mike, who was busily working a rotary saw, and had no intention of pausing for this visitor.

Brandon mouthed the word JIM to him.

Mike nodded toward a two-story shell of a building at the edge of the site.

Brandon gave a smile of thanks and made his way across the gravel.

Getting to the frame, he followed the rhythmic noise that came from the inside. Down a hallway still missing trim, past doorframes without doors, the beat grew louder with every step that Brandon took.

In one of what was to be a bedroom, Jim was dressed in overalls. He was hammering some drywall into place. The moment he noticed Brandon in the doorway, he audibly sighed.

"What the hell are you doing here?" he asked, not bothering to be polite.

Brandon stepped inside as the dust settled from Jim's hammering.

"I tried to call your house," he said. "But your phone's dead."

Jim kept working. "You came *all* the way out here to tell me that?" He hammered again.

"No, I want to ask you something about Linda."

"You wanna know if she snores, huh?" Jim gave a smirk.

Brandon turned to leave. "I should have known better than to come here."

Jim waved his hand. "Hey, hold on. I was kidding. Jeez. You *used* to have a sense of humor."

Brandon's expression didn't change. "Can you be serious for one damn minute? Please? It's important."

Jim put his hammer down by his side. "Sure, I can give it a shot."

"Do you know where Linda is right now?"

Jim didn't hesitate. "In class. What do I win?"

"No, Jim. She's not." Jim frowned.

Brandon continued. "She hasn't been to a single one of her classes all week."

"I thought you only had one class with her?"

"I asked around."

There was a beat. "I thought you were majoring in pre-law, not stalking."

"Don't get your bowels in an uproar," Brandon said, raising his hands. "Let me finish. Has she been acting strange lately?"

Jim looked more tired than angry at the question.

"What do you mean, strange?"

Brandon ticked items off with his fingers. "Nervous tension. Insomnia. Nausea. Erratic behavior."

"Uh, how did you know?" Jim asked, surprised.

"Has she been swearing a lot?"

Jim gave a dry smile. "Like a truck driver, why?"

"Oh no." Brandon exhaled, more out of realization than relief, and leaned back onto a windowsill. He looked dazed.

"Earth calling Brandon. Come in, Brandon."

Brandon looked up. "Jim, I think Linda's been using my Ouija."

Jim snorted. "Yeah... so what?"

"I know you think it's a crock of shit, but bear with me for a minute, okay?"

He held up a hand to pause any joke before it came. Jim kept quiet, knowing Brandon too well to think he could stop what was sure to be a mini lecture.

"When someone uses a Ouija board alone, like Linda's been doing, she becomes vulnerable. Susceptible to entities she may contact. At first, the spirit's helpful, even friendly. It lures her into using the board more often. Gets her hooked. Pretty soon, that's all she wants to do. Everything else, like school, sleep, food, it stops mattering. This is called Progressive Entrapment. The portal becomes more permanent. And those side effects — like the sudden swearing — that's the spirit working on her psyche. Breaking it down, wearing it thin. Like an infection in the brain.

Jim stared at him, not taking any of what he was saying in.

"Once she reaches that stage," Brandon continued, "the spirit changes. It starts to terrify her. Feeding on her fear once her will is low. Chipping away at her resistance. And when all resistance is gone, it moves in and takes total hold. That's how possession works."

Jim took a moment to wrap his head around the concept. "So, what you're telling me is... I'm living with Linda Blair. And she's swearing because the devil made her do it."

"This isn't a joke, I'm *serious*, Jim!"

"That's what makes it so funny. Weren't you the one who used to call this crap religious hysteria? I thought you were an atheist."

"I'm not saying it's a *demon*," Brandon snapped.

"Just the spirit of someone evil. Evil when they were alive. Evil now that they're dead. It's science not superstition. Energy doesn't die; it transfers." He took a breath. "Please, I want to bring a medium to the apartment. As soon as possible. Someone who can exorcise that spirit before anything bad happens."

"You're not serious..."

"Jim, how do you think I knew all those symptoms of Linda's?" Brandon asked. "They are *all* textbook entrapment! I spoke to my medium about it. She agrees it must be done now."

"And how much does she want to charge for such a great service, huh?"

Brandon rolled his eyes. "Jesus, Jim. You won't have to pay for it. I will!"

"You know those precious symptoms you listed? They also match pregnancy, Doctor Dumbass."

"What?" Brandon asked under his breath, genuinely taken aback.

Jim smiled at his old friend's shock. "Yeah, Linda's pregnant. I'm gonna be a father..."

"Okay, I guess..." Brandon said. Not sure of what to do now.

"Come on. Can't you try to be happy for us?"

Brandon looked up at Jim, trying to process the information. "Are you gonna marry her?" There was a pause.

Jim stared, basking in Brandon's turmoil at the news.

"Yeah... of course I am."

"You don't even love her."

"You haven't talked to me in years. So don't stand there and tell me what I Goddamn feel."

He picked up his new axe hammer and went back to work, pounding support nails into the drywall with a contained fury, much harder now, with a mounting frustration and anger behind each impact.

Brandon raised his voice over the pounding.

"I know you better than you think, Jim. Does Linda?"

The hammer strikes grew even louder as Jim put all of his anger and frustration behind each swing.

Brandon raised his voice to the point of almost screaming. "Because you knew you'd make a lousy doctor. Because you're not capable of giving a shit about anyone but yourself. And when you finally get tired of Linda..."

"Shut up, Brandon!" Jim yelled over the pounding.

But Brandon continued, "...You'll walk away. Just like you did with school. Just like you did with your parents. Just like you did with Susan!"

"Shut up!!!"

"But this time there'll be a baby! A baby you'll never be able to love! A baby you'll..."

Jim spun around to face Brandon, his knuckles white from squeezing his raised axe hammer so tightly. "I told you to SHUT UP!!!"

They stood a foot apart, chest to chest, tension rising between them.

"Jim?"

Both men turned to the voice.

Mike stood in the open doorway, watching them with a worried expression.

"There's a call for you in the foreman's trailer."

Jim didn't break eye contact with Brandon. "Take a message, Mike. I'm busy here."

Mike didn't flinch. "It's your landlady... something about Linda."

Jim's attitude changed. His anger dropped to worry, as he turned toward Mike.

"Is she okay?"

"I don't know," Mike shrugged. "I was just told to find you."

Jim dropped his hammer to the floor and ran out past them.

Jim barged through the foreman's trailer door, hard enough to make it slam into a filing cabinet against the wall. He went straight to pick up the phone, which lay off the cradle, on a pile of architectural plans.

"Hello?!" he said with a mounting dread.

Across town, in a too-warm kitchen filled with the smell of herbal tea, Linda sat hunched over a mug, both hands wrapped around the ceramic like the heat was the only thing sustaining her. Her face was still ghostly pale. One eye twitched slightly as she blinked.

Mrs. Moses held her telephone, her mouth pressed into a grandmotherly frown.

"Jim, this is Mrs. Moses."

'Is Linda alright?' came the reply.

"She's fine now," she explained. "But something up there scared her awful bad."

'Can I talk to her? Is she there?'

"Yes of course… here she is."

The phone exchanged hands with a soft clack.

Linda's hands trembled as she held the receiver.

"Jim?" she said weakly.

'I'm here, babe.'

"Oh God, Jim. It's David."

The name dropped like a weight into the conversation.

"David?"

'I don't know what happened to him. He used to be so nice…'

Jim was tight jawed as he listened to her shivering voice. *'And now… oh Jim, I'm so scared.'*

"All right," he said quietly. "I'm on my way home. I'll take care of it. I promise."

He hung up the phone and stood there, staring at the floor until a shadow moved behind him.

Brandon waited nervously.

Jim turned. His face was unreadable but without any want to say what he was about to say.

Then, low and calm, he opened his mouth, "I don't believe a word, but Linda does, and I'd do anything for her. Do you understand?" Brandon nodded.

"No matter what happened in the past, not with you or Susan or my parents or anyone else. I am with Linda. I am staying with Linda, and there is nothing you can do about it. Understand?" Before Brandon could answer, Jim added. "Bring your medium by tonight."

Later, the apartment looked like it had been decorated by a deranged scout troop with unlimited access to yarn and beer.

A round table had been dragged to the center of the living room, its surface empty but for a single lit candle. The bay window behind it was blocked off by a pyramid of empty Coke and Miller cans, stacked like a child's fortress. From wall to wall, strings had been crisscrossed in tight, purposeful angles, creating a web as small bells had been tied to each length at six-inch intervals. The slightest touch would send these bells jingling.

Jim buzzed Brandon into the building and then opened the front door to find him at the top of the stairs with the medium, and all the eccentricities she brought with her. With hair striped orange and green, torn fishnets, leather boots, rings on every finger, bubble gum snapping between her lips, she looked like the culmination of a dozen punk rock groupies being thrown into a blender. She couldn't have been more than twenty, but she carried herself like she'd already seen the other side and wasn't impressed by any of it.

"Jim," Brandon said, motioning to her. "This is Zarabeth, the best medium in Northern California."

She took Jim's hand and shook it with enthusiasm.

"Thanks for coming," Jim said with some uncertainty.

She paid no attention to his obvious hesitance. "Hey! Nice place. But you got yourself one gnarly spirit here. I can feel that much. See the hairs standing up on my arm?"

She shoved her arm in Jim's face, beaming her toothy grin, before skipping off to inspect the new decorations around the room.

Jim gave Brandon a sharp look as he whispered. "*This* is your expert? Where'd you find her, the damn circus?"

"Okay, fine'" Brandon replied. "She's a bit strange, I give you that."

"A *bit* strange? Her head's a friggin' rainbow!"

"She's on the level, trust me."

Jim wanted to tell them all to leave but stopped as Linda walked in from her nap in the bedroom.

Zarabeth turned to her enthusiastically. "Oh, *you* must be Linda," she beamed.

"Yes, I am."

"Bitchin'. Let's get this show on the road, shall we? No need to hang about."

Jim nodded toward the web of string and the card table. "We prepared everything just like Brandon told me."

"Rad job, Jim." Zarabeth said as she gave a little spin, admiring the handiwork. "As the kids would say, that's totally tubular."

Linda, still half asleep, took in the room, but before she could form a coherent thought, Zarabeth spoke up in a commanding tone.

"Okay, kill the lights. Jim, Linda... You guys grab a seat either side of me, okay? You two are the witnesses. Brandon, you go opposite. You will be the point of contact."

They moved through the web of string to the table, setting off a faint symphony of tiny bell chimes as they went. As Brandon flicked off the ceiling light, Zarabeth lit the candle in the center of the table. Now the only source of illumination, it threw long, disfigured shadows across the walls around them, which gave Linda a worried shiver.

She looked at Jim and motioned to the setup around them. "You did all this while I was asleep?" He nodded, almost embarrassed.

She smiled at him. "For me..."

Brandon took the last chair, bells chiming as he brushed by them, and they all sat where they were instructed.

The candle flickered lightly under their breath.

Zarabeth looked around the table with an uncharacteristic grimness.

"Okay. I'm gonna make contact now. So, whatever happens, stay in your seat, and keep quiet unless I say. I cannot stress that enough. If you stand or talk, the connection breaks. Brandon, you ask the questions that are needed, yeah?"

She then peered down in front of her and frowned.

"Oh, bummer. I forgot my damn crystal ball."

Jim rolled his eyes, to which Zarabeth snorted with laughter.

"Relax, Mr. Grumpypants," she said gleefully as she savored his reaction. "I don't *really* have a crystal ball. I'm messin' with ya. Just a little psychic humor, it helps break the ice."

Linda looked around the table before asking, "Shouldn't we join hands?"

Zarabeth crinkled her nose. "Nah. That's just in the horror movies," she said. "Anyway, my nails are too grody. Now, back to it. Let's talk to some ghosties."

Closing her eyes, she let her hands go flat against the table.

Jim and Linda stared at each other. Jim was unconvinced, and Linda was worried.

Brandon sat quietly, hands clasped on the table as he focused on Zarabeth.

The room soon fell silent, aside from the faint jingle of bells and the occasional creak from the building around them.

But it was only about twenty seconds until something happened...

The candle flickered violently, not from a draft, but in reaction to something else.

It then flickered the other way, as if the flame itself were being hit on one side, then the other.

Zarabeth's eyes snapped open, as she sat up straight as a rail.

As she did, Brandon's eyes lit up. He knew what was happening.

"Who are you?" he asked slowly and clearly.

There was silence as Zarabeth's lips started moving before she spoke.

"Please don't hate me," she said in a small, scared voice. Like a child's voice.

Brandon asked again, "*Who* are you?"

"...David."

Brandon glanced at Linda and Jim before turning back.

"David, do you know me?" he asked.

"Yes, Brandon. I know you."

"Can I ask how old you are?"

"Ten... I... I was... I was ten... when I..."

Brandon took a hesitant beat. "David, you have to tell me why you're doing all this to Linda. You're scaring her."

Zarabeth paused, before looking at Linda as she replied.

"I *love* Linda."

Brandon was not letting go of the questioning. "Then why are you terrorizing her, David?"

"She hurt my feelings. She won't talk to me anymore, because of... him."

"Jim?" Brandon asked. "You blame Jim?"

"He is so cruel. He said mean things about me."

Jim's mouth hung open, confused. "I said one thing drunk..."

Brandon spoke softly, "You're the one who's cruel, David. Threatening Jim and terrifying Linda"

Zarabeth's small voice wavered. "I'm sorry. I was angry. I don't want to hurt her." Zarabeth turned to face Linda. "I... I love you."

Linda looked away, getting teary-eyed.

Brandon spoke sharply. "Linda does not want you here anymore. I'm taking the Ouija home with me, where she can't get to it.

Zarabeth looked sad as she hung her head. "I know."

"The woman you're speaking through is a psychic," Brandon said. "She has the power to exorcise you from this apartment, you know that don't you?"

Zarabeth paused. "I'll go. I never meant any harm."

"David, why did you..." Linda asked, her voice wavering.

"I'm sorry," Zarabeth said, cutting her off. "Goodbye."

Linda stood up fast. "David, wait!"

"Linda! Don't!" Brandon shot out a hand.

Zarabeth's head flew back, and the candle flared, red and angry, filling the room with a blood-colored light. She then trembled with small rippling convulsions, her arms and legs seizing where she lay. The network of strings hanging around the table suddenly broke in three different places at once. As they did, the bells attached to them jingled loudly, then the pyramid of cans toppled over like they had taken a kick.

Jim rushed out of his seat, grabbed Linda and pulled her to him.

Brandon ducked as a string of bells nearly smacked into him.

Zarabeth fell forward, collapsing onto the table. As she did, on the same beat, the shutters at the window burst open, flooding the room with moonlight.

After one final pulse, the candle also snuffed itself out.

What followed was a long, terrible stillness, where Jim, Linda and even Brandon had no idea what they were supposed to do.

After a few moments Zarabeth raised her head and spoke in her own voice once more, dazed but grinning.

"Wow. I was right, that *was* pretty gnarly." She smiled at Brandon. "Get the lights, would ya?"

"Huh? Oh. Yeah..." Brandon said, looking stunned by all that had happened. He walked to the wall, flicking on the switch, and light returned to the living room like nothing had happened.

Shaking, Linda stepped forward and took Zarabeth's hand.

"Thank you."

Zarabeth smiled. "Too cool for school, but I didn't do squat. David left on his own steam."

"Well, that made little sense," Jim muttered.

Linda looked unsure. "Maybe I acted too quick."

Jim raised an eyebrow. "How do you mean? *If* that thing is real, it's an evil little prick who gets pissed at the slightest bullshit."

"David isn't evil," Linda said, glancing at Zarabeth. "Is he?"

"Unlikely." Zarabeth shrugged. "But I can't rule it out. He felt... scary."

Linda sounded hurt. "Maybe I should've given him another chance."

"No way," Jim said in exasperation. "Brandon's taking this thing home, and that's it. So, in the slightest chance any of this is not made up, then that'll solve it." He strode over to the sideboard, picked up the now-boxed Ouija, and handed it to Brandon.

Linda was still looking worried.

"We did the right thing," Brandon said to her. "Believe me, Linda. The last thing you want is for a spirit to tether itself to you."

"He's right," Zarabeth said. "That was one mondo ghost. Good thing the exorcism didn't happen. It would've been a mega-toughie. It—" She paused, as her expression fell, and she stared out blankly. "Oh no... I see a vision..."

Brandon looked worried. "What is it?"

Zarabeth then pointed toward the door. "Me... in your car... going home now." She burst out laughing at her own joke. "Just more psychic humor, guys. Come on, Brandon. Let's hit the musty dusty. Hang loose, stay cool, and don't forget your psychic humor. T. T.F.N., you beautiful people!"

She skipped over to the door, flung it open and left without another word.

Jim followed Brandon to the doorway.

"T. T.F.N.?" he asked.

"Ta-ta for now," Brandon replied, before turning to him. "Really, thanks for letting me bring her. I mean it. Thank you."

"Don't mention it." Jim gave a small smile. "To anyone... ever."

Brandon laughed and nodded as he disappeared down the stairs, taking the Ouija board with him.

Jim shut the door and leaned against it. He stared out across the wreckage of the room, the strings hanging loose, cans scattered, the candle melted.

Linda walked over and hugged him.

"So that little asshole says I'm cruel? Look at the mess he left us to clean up." he joked.

She didn't reply; she just smiled and kissed him on the cheek.

The streets leading away from the Lakewood Apartments were peaceful until Brandon's sports car roared by, its headlights shining across sidewalks and lawns as it sped faster than the law allowed.

Zarabeth was riding shotgun. Her rainbow appearance and the neon pink of her bubblegum were the only colors inside the black lined vehicle. She stared out the window, chewing with her mouth open, daydreaming as she occasionally blew a bubble so big it eclipsed her face before popping it with a wet snap. She then sucked it back and started over.

As they left the neighborhood and hit the parkway, Brandon looked across with the faintest smile. "You did a really good job tonight."

She kept watching the world pass by outside as she replied. "You ever heard the word malfeitor before?"

He raised a brow. "No. Should I?"

"I *think* it's a Portuguese word... maybe." She shook her head. "I don't know. I felt that word when I spoke to David. No idea why, but I'm sure it wasn't any good. Do you happen to know if David was Portuguese?"

"I don't think so."

Zarabeth hummed in her puzzled thoughts. "And he was *only* ten years old, right? You're sure?"

"Yeah, as much as I can be. Why what's wrong? That word?"

"Not just that. I felt that word over and over as he took hold. And it wasn't a normal grip... He must've taken mega-ghosty-vitamins, 'cause he was a real toughie. There was a cruelty in there somewhere... Ah, I dunno."

Brandon could sense genuine concern beneath her playfully spoken words. "Is it not over then?"

"Maybe..." All the playfulness was gone from her tone. "I see real bad danger ahead," she added.

"For Linda?"

"For you, if you miss my house." A mischievous

grin crept over her face, as she let out a laugh. "Because it's coming up on the right. Pull over, Jeeves!"

"More psychic humor, huh?" he muttered, not approving of her timing as he steered toward the curb.

She nodded, still chuckling.

The tires squeaked as the brakes kicked in.

Zarabeth opened the door and got out. Her smile dropped slightly as she looked back at him. "All kidding aside, though, something's hinky with all this. I gotta look into it."

"Like what?" Brandon asked, still holding the wheel.

"I'm not sure. Gonna look up that word and see anything that can explain that strength. Stay by the phone, and I'll call you later after I do the Nancy Drew bit. Something about that word malfeitor is familiar. Might not even be Portuguese! Something... I... I dunno. Anyway... T.T.F.N.!"

She waved as he drove away, her eyes following the taillights until they disappeared around the corner.

Inside his apartment, Brandon sat slouched on his couch.

The TV flickered with the grainy image of a black-and-white war film, that he paid little attention to. Instead, he was staring at the table in front of him. At the boxed Ouija board. Next to it sat his phone, which had been moved to be within arm's reach.

He reached to fluff a cushion under his arm. He

was not feeling patient enough to do anything except wait for Zarabeth's call, not that it would definitely come at this time of night, but sleep was the last thing on his mind.

* * *

The next morning, as the sun shone brightly, Linda looked out of the living room bay window. She was motionless, like a mannequin in a department store, looking out as if she were in a trance.

Backlit by sunlight that bled in all around her, the fabric of her robe drifted around her like smoke as it was carried on the small breeze.

Slowly turning back into her apartment, her eyes looked around with the sluggishness of someone still half-asleep. She peered down at the coffee table. It was bare. Missing something she was glad was now gone.

A sudden feeling sent a flash of dread creeping over her. Her eyes shot to the bedroom door—not pulled by any noise, but by a sudden knowing. As she stared at it, the door itself began to change. To grow. As though it were swelling or breathing.

Without a doubt or a fear for her own life, she stepped forward as if this were the most normal thing she could see. And as she got closer, the throbbing and growing door creaked open loudly, without her having to even touch it.

Walking through, she saw that the bed was made

and had not been slept in. The room was empty and heavily masked in thick, oily shadow.

Her gaze drifted dreamily over to her dresser.

It was there.

The Ouija board.

Not with Brandon. It was back, out of the box and laid out ready. The planchette, though, was missing. In its place, something else was there, embedded into the center of the board, and through the wood below. A handheld axe-hammer. It sat buried upright in the board; letters carved into its wooden handle. J.M.

Jim Morar.

Linda moved in closer, drawn to it, but through her daze felt a puzzlement at what it was doing here. Her hands reached out and pulled the tool free.

The initials on the handle almost gleamed at her. She stared at them before turning her glance back to the board. It seemed to be staring back up at her, as the gash in its middle resembled a lascivious smile.

Then the whole board cracked outward.

Through the axe-hammer's gouge, the board split as a huge, male hand shot up with an almighty *crash*, gripping her by the throat, digging its powerful fingers into her skin, breaking through the flesh and—

Linda woke with a scream, clutching at her neck, trying to pry away invisible hands she could feel tightening around it. Her sweat-covered body jolted. Her breath tore through her lungs, fast and uneven.

For a moment, she was lost in a daze of fear, unsure if she had truly escaped, or if she was actually hurt. She touched her neck again, dreading to feel the warm dripping of blood or the roughness of torn muscle. But there was no damage.

Slowly, her mind began to clear. It had been a dream, a terrible, horrifying one.

Disoriented, she looked around the now dark room, forcing herself into this reality fully.

It was not morning either like in her dream. It was still the middle of the night.

That's when she heard the noise in bed, beside her.

Jim was sprawled on his back. His loud snoring filled all the silence as he remained asleep obliviously.

Still trembling, Linda slid closer to him, seeking comfort in the warmth of his body. Curling against his side, she shut her eyes tightly, willing the remaining terror to fade away.

Zarabeth's two-storey apartment looked like a refuge for occultist hoarders. Old books were stacked in leaning towers across the floor and upon all pieces of furniture. Their cracked spines had titles printed on them, like *Cults of the U.S.*, *Demon Worship*, *Satanism in Practice*, and *Ouija*. This wasn't a mess though. There was a method and a filing system to it all. It was all her library that was perfectly ordered, in her mind anyway.

As the clock hit 2am, she sat in an old armchair,

surrounded by a selection of books that she had to research. Next to her, on the armrest, was a mug of coffee. A mug that had once been white was now the color of old bone, permanently stained brown on the inside.

From the stereo across the room, loud rock music rattled the dusty speakers, the distortion bouncing off walls. But there were no neighbors to complain. The rest of the building sat vacant and dark. The down-stairs, containing her occult and palm-reading shop, had long since closed for the night, its front windows blanketed in heavy velvet drapes. Here, in the quiet hum of isolation, Zarabeth thrived. She was a night owl by nature, and this world, cloaked in midnight and ritual, was hers alone.

The book in her lap was open to a page. The text on it was dense, but her attention was locked onto it with fascination. She barely blinked as she read slowly and carefully. She started to smile, having found the jackpot of information she had been looking for.

Reading all she needed to, she slammed the book shut, scattering butts from the ashtray as she jumped up. She did not care that she also knocked her cold mug of coffee over, sending it smashing onto the floor. She was too focused on what she had just learned, and too desperate to get to the phone to call Brandon.

She grabbed the receiver, excited, and started to dial, reading the number off a piece of paper taped to a cork board beside it.

As she got halfway through dialing, she suddenly froze.

Her smile dropped.

She sensed it.

That presence again.

The same one from Jim and Linda's apartment.

The room around her seemed to change without anything visibly altering.

As she turned, the walls seemed to stretch tighter. The air started to taste rotten and toxic. Something had shifted, she knew that much. Not a sound, not a shadow, just the world adjusting to another presence that should not be here.

She knew instantly what was happening. Few others would know the signs or feel it when reality started to tear. And from her research, she also knew what it was.

Then she saw it. Something beyond her vision. Something that was not physically in the room but altered the light as it passed in front of it.

"You," she shouted at the thing standing just beyond the veil.

The music from the stereo downstairs kept pounding loudly through the floorboards.

She knew she had to run, but whatever it was, it was standing between her and the door. She only had one way she could run... up the stairs.

Her bare feet hit the carpet at a run, until she got to the top and rounded the landing. The hallway in front of her was darker in a way she knew wasn't physical. It was unnatural.

She made it to her bedroom, hardly slowing as she raced in, sensing the thing close behind her. Reaching for her as it got near, grabbing at her.

She made it into the bathroom, where she slammed the door behind her. Locking it tight.

The noise soon started.

It wasn't fists on the other side of the door. It was much heavier. The door rattled in its frame, and hinges creaked under the assault.

Louder and louder, the pounding continued as the wood began to split apart.

Zarabeth, now petrified, backed up until her back hit the sink.

Her hands moved to her mouth, fingers clamping down to stifle the scream that started to escape her lungs.

Then, in an instant, the assault stopped. But as it did, it took all the other sound with it, even the music downstairs.

There was nothing.

Just silence, an unnatural silence.

Reality had broken around the room.

She waited, listening. She knew that thing was still there.

Five seconds.

Ten.

Fifteen.

Still silence.

Slowly, she took a step forward, then another. Her eyes stayed on the door in front of her, too afraid to look away.

She held her hand out to grab the handle. She knew her only choice was to run. She could not let herself be trapped in this room. If that thing was outside, maybe she could run past it and get out of the building... *Maybe...* But she didn't make it to the handle.

Something moved by the window.

She didn't hear it happen. She felt it.

A blade across her throat.

Then came the pain.

Her gargled scream would not be heard by anyone.

There were no neighbors to call the cops, or passersby at this time of night.

The edge of her vision went red, as her throat split, opening her neck up. Blood arced over the bathroom door in a wide, thick torrent.

Her knees buckled, and she dropped hard onto the laminate floor, hands flailing uselessly at the air, trying to stop what had already happened. Her mouth opened but only a vomit of the darkest arterial blood came out.

She didn't have time to collapse any more, as in that next moment, she felt her body being wrenched backward and the window to the bathroom shattered.

Like a doll leaving trailing red ribbons, her body careened through the air and fell toward the ground.

The picket fence didn't break. It took her collision

easily. The pointed posts pierced through her body with horrible ease. One through her thigh. One through her belly. One through her heart. And one went through her head.

Her body jerked once.

The silence soon returned, but it was a natural silence now. One where the night sounds of a distant city could be heard, as well as the loud music from inside her apartment.

Chapter Six

Brandon was still on the couch, lying half on, half off, face mashed into the armrest as he began to wake after a nightmare-fueled sleep.

The television was still on, but the old films were gone, and in their place was the early morning news. Its chiming jingle stirred him out of his sleep.

A plastic-faced anchorman recited the latest disaster with all the empathy of a robot reading a grocery list, complete with a jarringly confident smile.

"...Police are calling it the worst traffic accident in the county's history," he said with an upbeat tone.

Brandon wiped the dried drool from around his mouth, then rubbed his eyes, as he adjusted to being awake once more.

He shivered. The blinds were drawn just enough to let in slices of gray morning, but not enough to warm the room around him, and he felt every degree of it.

As he moved, the couch creaked beneath his

weight, and when it did, the tone of the news also changed to a more somber timbre.

"An accident of a different sort claimed the life of a Fairfield resident late last night, when she fell to her death from a second-story window."

Brandon took notice upon hearing his town's name. Normally, even the local news was filled with stories from LA or San Francisco, but Fairfield? That was rare.

The phone was already in Brandon's hand. He didn't remember picking it up in his sleepy state, but realized he had when he was already halfway through dialing.

"The victim, Sara Crawford, also worked as a professional medium under the pseudonym of Zarabeth." The name hit him hard.

He stared at the screen as he stopped dialing. There, in case he thought he might have misheard the name, was a picture of the victim. It was her. The multi-colored hair, the attitude, staring out of the photograph on screen, straight at him.

Whatever the reporter said after was lost on him. Something about an ongoing investigation. Suicide not ruled out. Police unsure. Brandon couldn't say, as he had stopped listening, and his focus had moved to the Ouija board. The box was still sitting on the table in front of him. Still exactly where he'd left it.

He leaned forward and lifted its lid. Maybe he could contact her?

He stared in shock.

The board and planchette were missing from the box.

He *knew* Jim packed them. He saw him do it.

The intercom repeatedly buzzed in the apartment. Impatient and incessant.

Jim walked toward the door in a bathrobe, hair a bush of messiness, his breath still ripe with the stench of morning. He slapped the intercom button.

"What the hell do you want?"

"Jim, it's Brandon. We have to talk, right now." Jim glanced at his watch.

7:04am.

It was too early for this to be anything good, and too early for Brandon to be playing around. "All right. I'll buzz you up."

"No, Jim," Brandon quickly said. "You gotta come down here. I can't risk coming up."

The pause on the line became uncomfortable as Jim tried to make sense of what was being asked.

"On my way," he mumbled, grabbing his shoes, trying to be as quiet as he could, to not wake Linda.

Brandon stood on the other side of the glass door, hands buried in the pockets of the same clothes he had slept in. He was a shadow of the well-groomed and well-dressed man he liked to portray.

The door opened, and Jim walked out into the cold, pulling his bathrobe tighter around him.

"Okay, I'm here," he said. "What's up that you had to drag me down this early?"

Brandon didn't ease into it. "Where's Linda?"

"Still asleep. Why?"

"Because Zarabeth's dead," as Brandon said those words, he frowned as if he were the one being told it.

"What? How?"

Brandon could barely bring himself to believe what he was saying. "Fell out a window, apparently," he said. "Or pushed by someone. Or suicide. Police don't know yet."

"Christ..." was all Jim could say. He had met her only hours before. He didn't much like her, but the fact that she was now dead made him feel numb. Since his parents died, every death had hit him the same. When Susan died, when Lloyd died... he felt sad, but that was it. He didn't feel the actual grief. With Zarabeth too.

"I don't think it was an accident," Brandon continued. "She was looking into David and what she felt last night."

"What she felt?" Jim struggled to believe this wasn't all some sort of sick joke. It seemed all too unreal.

"She said something didn't feel right about any of it. She was going to dig into it more... and I... I think she found out something and David killed her to keep her quiet."

Jim crossed his arms, already having alarm bells

ringing in his mind. "The *spirit* killed her." He said in disbelief.

"Yeah, I am serious. And I think he cut your phone line too. I tried calling Linda to stop using the board, then the phone went dead. Then you were electrocuted. David said quite clearly last night that he didn't like you. And as for Lloyd... I think David was aiming for you, but he missed."

Jim closed his eyes slowly for a second. Trying desperately to wrap his head around this entire unbelievable concept. "Brandon, do you even hear yourself? You're telling me that a ten-year-old ghost is flying around Fairfield killing people? Come on!"

"I know it sounds crazy. But it's the only thing that makes any kind of sense."

Jim didn't answer, but his silence wasn't agreement.

"I'm *sure* I'm right," Brandon added.

"Okay," Jim replied. "Let's say you are. That it's all a ghost's fault. Why now? Why did he wait so long? You contacted him first. Long before Linda ever touched that thing."

"But I've never used it alone," Brandon said. "I always had someone with me. Zarabeth was there most of the time. You're never supposed to use it alone. Never. It's what I was *trying* to tell Linda. But David cut your phone line."

"But you took the board, so what's the problem?"

"I checked the box this morning. It was empty. The board's gone."

"That's impossible. I packed it, and I saw you take it."

"Linda must have removed it again when we weren't looking. She's obsessed with it, Jim. You've seen it. She's already in the progressive entrapment stage. She denied it when I asked her, and got really defensive, like a junkie. First pleading, then lying, then bargaining. It's all the same."

Jim sighed. "You don't have to make this any more difficult. If she does have it, I'll just have to find it and get rid of it. Simple."

"Simple? No Jim, you don't get it. It's too late for that," Brandon said. "She's open now. David doesn't need the board anymore."

"I thought that's how he got in. The board. That's where he got his power from... and that's why you're here. Because the board isn't with you. Why do you care if it's not needed?" Jim was starting to lose his patience, and his voice was starting to rise. "You think she took it. If he doesn't need it, why would she bother taking it at all? It doesn't make any sense."

"Jim, she was going through withdrawals. She probably doesn't even know that David is tethered to her now. And the board doesn't give him power. It's just a portal. Spirits are trapped in their own world and can't enter ours without an anchor or channel, like... like a medium, or a Ouija... Or someone who's been opened by progressive entrapment."

Jim didn't like the sound of it. "So, Linda's become his portal."

Brandon nodded. "And eventually, he'll possess her."

The word 'possess' made Jim scoff. None of this was real to him. None of it was logical in his mind. It couldn't be.

Brandon continued. "We have to stop him... That's why I'm going to Tahoe."

"Tahoe? What the hell's in Tahoe?"

"That's where David said he died. I need to check it out. If we're going to stop him, we need to know who he really was. For all I know, he's been lying to me since the first time I contacted him."

He stepped backward, off the porch.

Jim was still in a state of disbelief, mainly that Brandon of all people believed all this. "You're really going there? To ghost hunt?"

"I have to... I feel responsible."

"When are you leaving?"

"I just gotta go pack some things..." He started walking away. "Just keep an eye on Linda. Please."

"Hey..." Jim called out after him. "I don't believe any of this. But... good luck and... be careful, okay?"

Jim held his hand out, much to Brandon's surprise.

Brandon walked back, they both smiled politely and shook hands. After a moment, they broke off, feeling equally self-conscious. Remembering that they were no longer friends.

And with that, Brandon left.

Jim stood in the doorway, watching him drive away.

He then noticed something else on the street. A car was parked further down. Lieutenant Dewhurst sat behind the wheel, staring back at him.

"Are you shitting me?" Jim muttered as he walked back into the house.

Linda sat on the side of the bed. She had waited for Jim to leave the house, and as soon as he went out to speak to Brandon, she had gone to the closet and brought out the Ouija board and planchette that she had hidden in there.

She felt bad for stealing from Brandon and knew that she would be found out. But to her, this was too important. She had to speak to David, to find out what happened and why. *He's just a little boy, after all,* she thought to herself.

The board was placed carefully on her knees. The planchette on top, her fingers hovering over it, with only the most minimal of contact.

"David?" she called again for the tenth time this morning. "Please answer? Can you hear me?"

No movement from the planchette. No answer.

She placed both hands on it, as gently as she could manage. "Have you come back? Are you here, David? I *need* to talk to you. Please." Still nothing.

She felt a shiver of apprehension as she tried to remain calm and not let any of this derail her emotionally.

"David, please. If I mean anything to you, just answer me."

No reply.

"Please. Please. *Please.*" Nothing. Linda removed her fingers from the planchette and placed the Ouija on her dresser.

"Fine," she whispered. "I'll just have Jim get rid of it."

The planchette then jumped to life, sliding across the board of its own accord.

NO.

Linda gasped loudly, her breath knocked out of her.

Her eyes stared down, as she let loose a stifled cry of fear.

David had been there the whole time listening to her, spying on her.

Jim had just stepped through the door when the scream from the bedroom reached him. Blood curdling and unmistakably Linda's. It shot out so sharply that he had no time to question or overthink it. He ran as fast as he could down the hallway.

Before he could get within a foot of the bedroom door, it shut in his face with an almighty *slam.* Then, from the other side, he heard Linda screaming for him.

"*Jim, help me!*" came her plea.

He grabbed the door handle. It wouldn't move.

Wouldn't turn, wouldn't even rattle. As if it had been welded shut.

From inside came more screaming. Linda's desperate cries. And between them, the sound of furniture scraping against the floor.

Jim banged on the door. "Linda! Let me in!"

But she was in no state, and let loose another scream, followed by a thud, then a howl of pain.

He stared at the door. He had no choice.

He kicked the lock hard.

The door cracked loudly, but the wood still held together.

Another kick.

Another.

A fourth.

A fifth.

Each kick was strong and used all of Jim's might. The door cracked more with each blow.

The sixth kick broke the wood inward. The door snapped into two large, splintered pieces.

He charged inside, as the door fell apart, and Linda was thrown across the room by an invisible force. She crumpled against the far wall, her body smashing against it. She fell and slumped to the floor in a heap.

Jim was beside Linda in seconds. Without stopping to consider what had done this to her, he crouched and lifted her off the floor, carrying her onto the bed.

Her head lolled back. Her face was gray and waxy, her eyes fluttering in and out of consciousness.

He felt her pulse as he studied his watch. He

checked the dilation of her pupils. Not that he was any kind of doctor but knew enough from his limited medical education to see the warning signs. Linda was reactive, but sluggish and unable to stay focused.

Out of the corner of his eye, he saw it... the Ouija board. It sat innocently on the dresser.

He grimaced. Despite his disbelief, he couldn't help but feel the board was to blame. Logic told him otherwise, but something deeper, irrational, pulled at him.

Brandon, Zarabeth, and Linda all believed in it. And even though he didn't, he still harbored a deep, unshakable hatred for that board. Against his better judgment, he stood and rushed toward it. He picked it up with both hands, staring at the printed letters like they might suddenly speak, like the board might reveal something, or do something.

"Jim? Linda? Is everything all right?" He looked up from the board.

Mrs. Moses was peering into the open front door in the living room, surrounded by three other tenants from the apartment building. They were clustered like birds around a feeder, peering in with a mix between curiosity and caution.

"What's going on?" she called out. "We heard all the banging... Jim? Linda? Are you there?"

Jim walked out of the bedroom, still gripping the board and planchette in his hand. A look of anger on his face.

"Mrs. Moses, call an ambulance, now."

"Wh-what h-happened?" she stuttered.

"Linda's unconscious," he said. "Please hurry…"

With just a nod, she turned and rushed down the stairs. Leaving the other tenants who still lingered, staring in.

"You hear all that screaming?" One of them whispered.

"I'll bet he beat her," another muttered in reply.

They spoke to each other, thinking that Jim could not hear what they said. But he could. He just didn't react. He didn't even look at them. He just walked across the room to the bay window, opened it wide, and hurled the board out into the daylight, down into the side alley below.

The Ouija fell from the second floor, flipping itself, before it came crashing into the metal lip of the dumpster. Landing inside. The planchette missed and fell to the lawn beside it.

From down the street, Lieutenant Dewhurst watched from behind the wheel of his sedan. His curiosity piqued, he leaped out of his car and jogged over to the house.

With Jim back in the apartment and no one looking out anymore, Dewhurst quickly crossed the lawn over to the dumpster.

There, the Ouija board sat, open and face up.

Dewhurst stared at it baffled, as the approaching sirens could be heard in the distance.

The ambulance howled through the streets of Fairfield as it approached the emergency bay of the hospital. Its siren and lights in full effect.

A couple of hours later, inside the waiting room, it was silent, several listless people suffering the endless wait to be seen. Each was either wounded, in pain, or waiting with someone who was.

Just outside the entrance, in the smoking area, Jim sat hunched forward on a small plastic chair, cigarette burning between his fingers, ash hanging off the end. He had not taken a drag since he first lit it up. He was too distracted as his mind spun.

Finally dropping the unsmoked butt to the floor, he walked back inside. There, waiting on one of the chairs, was Lieutenant Dewhurst, reading a book about juggling, with his open bag of oranges on the chair next to him.

Jim had wanted to keep quiet, ignore the policeman and just be here for Linda, but as he paced the waiting room worriedly, he could not help but feel Dewhurst's eyes following him. Judging him.

And as the tension grew, Jim was the first to break as he strode over to where the policeman was sitting.

"What the hell do you want from me, huh?" He demanded. "Why're you watching my apartment? Why the hell are you even *here*?"

Dewhurst never looked up from his book. "Y'know, I don't think I have the dexterity for juggling." He turned, picked out three oranges from the bag beside him, and in silence attempted to juggle them. The fruit immediately tumbled to the floor. Dewhurst shrugged, picked them up, and put them back in the bag, quickly returning his attention to his book. "It's quite annoying really."

Jim stood there, confused and sick of whatever charade the cop was playing. He reached down, grabbed the book, and hurled it across the waiting room.

Dewhurst got to his feet in mock indignation. "My, that was very rude of you."

"Yeah, I got a 'D' in manners," Jim snorted. "Now what the hell are you playing at?"

There was a tense silence as the two men stared at each other. Then Dewhurst adopted a calm tone; his method had worked; he had managed to put his suspect on the back foot. "Okay... How well did you know Sara Crawford?" he asked

"What? Who?' Jim asked, "Was she into juggling too?"

"Did you know her or not?"

Jim shook his head. "I've never heard of her."

"She used the pseudonym 'Zarabeth' sometimes."

Jim's surprised expression gave him his answer.

The lieutenant continued. "I don't know about how much she liked juggling, but she did manage to get her throat slit *before* she went headfirst through her bathroom window. That's a pretty neat trick, I guess. Do you know what it was cut with?

Jim tried his best to not show his shock. "You're going to say a hatchet, aren't you?"

Dewhurst nodded, "The striation marks and trace metal on her throat exactly match those on the ropes at your construction site, proving they were both cut with the same type of weapon. Hatchet or Axe-hammer."

He paused a moment to let that sink in. Jim didn't reply. He just stared back.

Dewhurst smiled. "Y'know, I once saw this magician make an entire elephant disappear. An entire elephant! And that's no mean feat. I mean, even a baby elephant would be pretty hard to just slip up your sleeve. Of course, I know he didn't really make that elephant disappear..." He leaned forward, whispering conspiratorially. "He just managed to hide it somewhere. I do hope you find your axe-hammer." Walking over to the other side of the room, he retrieved his book from the floor, then returned holding it up. "This is a good book by the way, I recommend it."

Jim was growing tired of this. "Your department's had that site locked down for days." He stated. "Why haven't *you* found anything yet?"

"We will... Eventually." Dewhurst said, sitting back in his chair. "That reminds me, I went to your work earlier today. Foreman showed me all the jobs you've been working on. Can you tell me what you've been using to hang that sheet rock stuff?"

"Three-inch nails."

"Are you trying to be funny?"

"No, sir," Jim replied sarcastically. "I wear a big red nose and bright, baggy pants when I'm trying to be funny."

Dewhurst stared at him, unamused. Jim continued.

"Look, I'm sure you've already checked all my credit card receipts, and you know I bought a new axe-hammer two days after..." He took a breath. "After the accident... So, are we done now?"

Dewhurst didn't get a chance to reply as Doctor Morton walked in. No nonsense, dressed in a pristine, white coat, and holding a clipboard, she caught Jim's stare, nodding at him.

"James Morar?" she said.

Jim crossed to her, worried. "Yes?"

She did not offer any smile as she walked over. "My name is Doctor Morton," she said matter-of-factly. "I am the attending doctor for Linda Brewster."

"How is she, doc?"

Morton nodded as she looked at her clipboard. "It appears that your diagnosis was right on the money. She has a concussion. That must've been quite a fall, no?"

He nodded, feeling worried. "How about the baby?"

The doctor hesitated. "Well, Ms. Brewster missed her appointment here with her obstetrician yesterday... So, they didn't get to hear the news. But I can tell you that she is not pregnant, nor has she ever been."

Jim didn't know what to think. "But... but she's

been having morning sickness," he said, as if sharing this information with the doctor could magically change the results.

"Nevertheless, she is not pregnant. No matter what symptoms she may have exhibited. It may have been a phantom pregnancy."

Jim paused and looked around helplessly, even at Dewhurst, who just kept quiet. "Can I see her?" Jim asked.

"Of course you can." Dr. Morton motioned to the door to the wards. "But Ms. Brewster is still unconscious."

As Jim started to walk away, Dewhurst called out after him.

"Mr. Morar," he said, "Before you go, can you let me know where you were last night?"

Jim didn't even turn back as he replied. "Ask your wife, Lieutenant."

Dewhurst nodded and could not help but smile. "I'll speak to you soon," he said.

"Whatever," Jim replied, disappearing through the door into the wards.

Linda was asleep in her hospital bed. The I.V. bag that hung on a stand fed fluids directly into her arm. Its slow *drip, drip, drip* loudly ticked off the seconds as they passed. The white sheet covering her rose and fell along with her shallow breaths.

Jim was sitting in a chair beside her. He didn't say a

thing. He could only stare at her and feel a well of guilt. Not that he did this, but that he could not stop it from happening.

Under the room's harsh, sterile light, her skin appeared almost translucent, as delicate blue veins traced faint lines beneath its surface.

The machines in this room didn't beep or flash like Jim had seen in the movies. Here they just sat, quietly displaying incoherent numbers. He tried to understand what they meant, so that he may be able to figure all this out. But it was useless. He did not stay in school long enough to learn about any of this.

He hung his head and, for the longest time, did not move.

He just sat, dwelling on everything that happened.

When Jim did eventually look up, his expression was no longer one of sadness or mourning, but one of grim determination. He had to fix this. Somehow.

He stood up and kissed Linda on the forehead before walking out of the room.

The small travel bag zipped shut, full of overnight clothing and toiletries. Brandon stared down at it, steeling himself for what he was about to do.

His apartment had not been touched since he woke up. The curtains were still drawn, the television still on. He had raced over to Jim and Linda's apartment to check on them, then come straight back to pack. He should have just driven to Tahoe already. He could have picked up toiletries at a gas station on the way. Why did he even come back here? Did he really need to pack?

He knew the answer. One that he would never admit. He was scared. His one guide in all this was dead. And she was not the only one who had been killed. And stupidly, he had put it upon himself to try and save the day? Was it really from a guilty conscience? None of it would have happened if it weren't for him.

He grabbed the bag and, forcing himself to move, walked over to the door and opened it.

Jim was there, with a look of surprise, his hand raised, ready to knock.

Brandon flinched, startled. "What the hell are you doing here?"

"I'm going with you," Jim didn't ask, he just said.

"But where's Linda?"

"I'll tell you on the way."

Chapter Seven

The sports car cut across the highway like a bullet. The sun beat down on its silver surface, reflecting brightly as it sped along the flat, straight road, passing the scrub and dry hills that stretched out on either side.

The engine roared as the pedal was pressed all the way down.

Inside, Jim held a road map open across his lap. His finger traced routes while Brandon kept his eyes on the road ahead.

The highway was mostly empty, apart from the occasional vehicle that passed in the other direction and quickly disappeared in the rearview.

"You really think she'll be okay?" Brandon asked. "She's all alone in that hospital."

"What can I do? I threw the board away, that's all I could do... and I can't stop anything coming for her anyway, can I? In fact, I seem to make it worse. That thing hates me."

Brandon shrugged.

"Let's say David comes back. So, me being there would logically be the worst thing for her. It's better that I'm here trying to solve the problem, instead of being there and putting a target on her back."

"I guess so," Brandon replied. "I just hope she's okay."

"She will be. Anyway, when we get there, what's the plan?" Jim didn't take his eyes off the map. "What's our first move? Where do we need to go?"

"I thought about that... We should go to the public library."

"The library? Why?"

"Why not?"

"Oh, that's good then..." Jim said. "As long as you've got a watertight reason."

Outside, a green sign blurred past the windows. In large letters it said:

NOW LEAVING FAIRFIELD CITY LIMITS
Thank you for visiting... We'll miss you!

Three hours later, the car was parked on the banks of Lake Tahoe, in the lot at the Public Library.

It was a large timber-built building that looked less like a library and more like an oversized hunting lodge. "You sure this is the place?" Brandon asked as they looked at the building through the windscreen.

Jim pointed to the door. "You do see that big sign, right?"

Indeed, above the door, as clear as day, a blue and yellow sign proudly stated *Tahoe City Public Library*.

The whole journey had been like this. When either of them said something, it was met with sarcasm or insult. But at each instance, neither of them took it any further. Even when they were still friends they'd been the same.

The library smelled like disinfectant as a cleaner mopped the hardwood floors in front of them. The sun, now at its apex, shone through the many tall windows around the building, highlighting all the dust particles that swamped the air. So much of it that Brandon started to breathe shallower, inhaling as little as possible.

The bookshelves ran tall and wide across the whole library, aside from the line of microfiche machines that sat at the far end. Next to them, a set of metal shelves, each packed with large black folders.

Brandon nodded in that direction. "We gotta check the old newspapers for any mention of David's accident."

"Oh right!" Jim said, quickly realizing the plan. "You could have just told me in the car!"

Each of them soon walked across the room and took a machine each.

"You know how long it'll take us to go through

every newspaper printed in 1955?" Jim said without looking up.

"We don't need all of them," Brandon replied. "Just go to the ones from that August. That's when David claims that he died. August 7th."

With a large microfilm folder open between them, they had taken a film each and begun searching.

The reels clicked softly as they scrolled through grainy black-and-white headlines. Looking for any relevant articles.

"You said they lie," Jim said. "So, what makes you think this isn't all bullshit and he just led us here?"

"Oh, you're a believer now, are you?"

Jim didn't know what he believed. He just knew he didn't *want* to believe. After he had seen Linda thrown across the room by something that wasn't even there, he knew better than to just discount the impossible theories, if rationality could not answer it.

Their machines kept whirring as scans flicked past on the monitors, one page at a time.

It was in the fourth film they had looked at that Jim stopped scrolling.

"Oh, hello there," he said with a smile.

Brandon peered over. "What? You found anything?"

"Hold on a second. I'll enlarge it."

Quickly, the headline of the paper zoomed in and

filled the monitor: *BOY DIES IN BOATING ACCIDENT*.

"Oh wow... That's gotta be it, right?" Brandon asked.

Scrolling down to the article. Jim read the first few lines to himself.

"Bingo! This is it!" He then read it aloud. "Tragedy struck early Tuesday morning when a gasoline explosion aboard a small motorboat on Lake Tahoe's north side claimed the life of 10-year-old David Simpson."

"Guess he wasn't lying then," Brandon said. "What else does it say?"

Jim continued to read from the screen, "The incident occurred shortly after sunrise while the boat was docked at a private jetty. Emergency crews arrived soon after, but David was pronounced dead at the scene. The cause of the explosion remains under investigation by local authorities. David was the only child of John and Betty Simpson, long-term residents of the area. Funeral services will be held this Saturday at Holy Spirit Cemetery. The family has asked for privacy as they grieve the loss of their son."

They sat back in silence taking it all in.

Brandon finally spoke, "Okay, so we now know he did die here, exactly how he said and when he said. Also, we have confirmed how old he was." He thought for a moment. "But it still doesn't explain *why* he's targeting Linda. Or why he has it in for you."

"Okay. So, how do we find all that out? You tried asking him. That failed miserably."

"Maybe," Brandon spoke as he thought aloud. "Maybe we ask his parents about him? Say we are writing a paper on accidents in the lake or some shit. Try and get them to tell us what he was like?"

"That won't help!"

"Well, there's not much else we can do is there?" Brandon then stood up. "There's a phone outside. Come on."

The glass telephone booth reeked of urine, and so much worse.

Both Jim and Brandon stared at it with disgust.

Braving it out of necessity, Brandon reached out and grabbed the directory that hung from a chain on the wall. Pulling it as far out as it would reach, he opened the damp, ripped pages and flicked through them, stopping when he found the S section. Slowly turning the pages, his finger ran down the column until it rested on SIMPSON. He slowly looked at each entry.

"Damn," he muttered, slamming the directory closed and letting it drop on the chain. "There's no listing for a John or Betty Simpson."

"Wait, that article said David was buried at the Holy Spirit Cemetery, yeah?"

"Yeah?"

"So maybe the caretaker has an address on an invoice or something. I mean, you gotta have a contact for a grave, right? In case of... stuff. I don't know. But sounds like an option."

"All right," Brandon looked at him, impressed. "That's actually a good idea."

As they headed back to the car, Brandon kept wiping his hands on his jeans, clearly unsettled by whatever might've been on that filthy directory. Jim looked at him with an amused smirk.

"I may not know about cemeteries, but you wanna take a guess at what I *do* know?"

"What?" Brandon asked, still distracted.

"Libraries... And the fact that inside, they have all the phone directories, in pristine condition."

Brandon stopped. "And why didn't you say anything?"

"And miss the floorshow?" Jim laughed.

By the time they got to the cemetery, the sun had already set and left the sky a dark orange hue. The rusted gates in front of them bore the name *Holy Spirit Cemetery* in flaking golden paint.

Brandon was sitting in the car with the headlights dimmed, watching as Jim came walking back from the caretaker's cottage.

"Well?" Brandon asked as the door opened, and Jim peered in.

"Well, nobody's home."

Brandon sighed. "Well, I guess we'll have to come back tomorrow, won't we?"

"As long as we're here, we should take a look at David's grave," Jim said, nodding toward the gate.

"Why?"

Jim smiled. "Why not?"

He shut the car door without another word.

By the time Brandon switched the engine off and got out, it was too late. Jim had already climbed the wall and was going over the top.

"Hey, come back!" he called out. "We could get in trouble."

But Jim was already over the wall and had dropped out of sight.

Brandon checked the street behind him. There was no one around to see what they were doing.

"I got a bad feeling about this," he mumbled, as he reluctantly followed.

The cemetery was dark and cold. Much colder than it had been outside the gates. Within its stone walls, the air bit at them and tasted stale to breathe.

The large trees lining the area only allowed for thin slivers of moonlight to fall onto the graves, making it difficult to see much, and for every thrown shadow to look like some kind of monster lying in wait.

Brandon dropped down from the wall and looked around, his eyes full of trepidation. All he could see were dark, empty rows of headstones stretching out in all directions.

"Jim?" He called in a hushed voice.

No one answered.

"*Jim?* Where the hell are you?"

Slowly, he stepped forward, moving through the rows carefully, his eyes taking a while to adjust to the dark.

Around him, the wind had picked up, stirring the settled dry leaves, and sending them tumbling past him.

"It's like a damn horror film," he grumbled to himself.

Then, as if on cue, a *crack*.

A twig breaking underfoot. Not his foot.

He stopped in his tracks.

"Jim?" he whimpered, filled with an immediate dread.

Another *crack*. Much closer this time. Then another. They were footsteps, and they were headed right toward him.

He held his breath. Of course, he knew it *had* to be Jim. But with all the talk of ghosts, and being on the grounds of the resting dead, he expected much, much worse to appear.

The footsteps came closer.

Brandon spun around, gritting his teeth. Expecting everything bad that could be possible.

There was nothing. Only gravestones and darkness.

Suddenly, a hand shot out and grabbed him by the shoulder.

He yelped in fear and twisted around to see— Jim.

Of course, Jim.

"Will you stop making so much noise?" Jim hissed,

clearly amused by Brandon's discomfort. "You're gonna get us both arrested as grave robbers."

Brandon's pulse was speeding as he stared at Jim "You scared the shit out of me you prick! Where *were* you? I called out for you!"

Jim pointed behind him. "I found someone I want you to meet."

"The caretaker?"

Jim smiled, though not in humor. "David's parents."

The three headstones sat side by side under an unbroken shine of pale moonlight. The one in the center, was older and more weather-beaten. It simply read:

DAVID SIMPSON
OCT. 16, 1945 – AUG. 11, 1955

Flanking it were two newer slabs, new enough that the earth in front of them had barely settled yet. The names on them were no less unsettling:

JOHN SIMPSON
MAY 21, 1926 – MAR. 06, 1985

BETTY SIMPSON
SEPT. 05, 1931 – MAR. 06, 1985

Jim stared at the etching, his voice quiet. "Look at the dates. His parents died on the same day... Less than three weeks ago."

Brandon stood beside him. "Must've been some kind of accident, right?"

"After all that's happened to us... You really think it could be an accident?"

They turned to each other with a worried look.

The 480 Motel was a cheap two-story building along an empty stretch of the roadside, set outside the city limits.

Brandon's car was parked outside one of the rooms, where the light inside glowed out from behind the thick, dusty curtains.

The room was all they could find at this hour, and at its low rate, neither of them were surprised by how dirty it was. The sheets on the twin single beds were watermarked. The walls were nicotine yellow. The carpet, well, it should never be stood on with bare feet. But neither Jim nor Brandon seemed to care. They had larger issues to contend with.

Jim lay sprawled on one of the beds, shoes off, arms crossed behind his head. Brandon unpacked his bag, placing each item into the rickety drawers as if he were staying longer than a single night.

"We should try to get some sleep," Brandon said, but his voice lacked conviction.

Jim nodded to the ceiling. "Yeah, that's likely."

Brandon closed the drawer. "First thing tomorrow, I want to get out to the dock where the accident happened."

"It already *is* tomorrow," Jim said.

Brandon didn't respond, he just picked up his toiletries bag.

Jim saw this and sat up. "Don't suppose you've got a spare toothbrush in there do ya?" Brandon shook his head.

"Damn. I hate talking to ghosts with plaque on my teeth." He waited, before adding, "Just a little psychic humor there."

They laughed despite everything, not just at the bad joke, but at all of it.

Then they stopped.

"God. Why are we laughing?" Brandon said, exhaling loudly.

"Guess it helps us forget how scared we are."

The silence that followed was awkward, as they stared at each other.

Becoming somewhat self-conscious, Brandon took his toiletry bag into the bathroom and placed it on the sink.

When he came back in, Jim was sitting up on the edge of the bed.

"What happened to us, Brandon?" he said softly. "We used to be like brothers. We..." He didn't finish his thought.

Brandon looked away as he walked around the side of his bed. "Things change. People change. Everything changes. Just what it is. Took me a while to come to terms with that after all that happened."

"It was bad enough after Susan... But when I started seeing Linda..." Jim watched as Brandon sat on his bed.

Brandon hesitated before he spoke. "I... I know... But every time I see the two of you together, I go crazy. I start saying stupid things, and I can't stop. I tell myself, '*Stop being an asshole*,' but then my mouth opens and out comes another stupid remark."

"Well, you were right," Jim said as he lay back on the bed. "Remember what you said about me quitting school?"

"I'm sorry."

"Don't be... You know what I did... I hid from it. After Susan... She blamed me... and why not? I was an asshole. I should never have been with her in the first place. But Linda, I don't think it's the same. But I know I don't deserve her." He took a deep breath in. "If I had any real guts, I'd get out of her life before she wastes any more time on me."

"She loves you."

Jim shrugged. "I make her laugh, that's all."

"So do I. That's hardly a reason to be with you. Otherwise, she'd rather be with me."

"I guess..." Jim said with a smile. "But I don't fumble and whimper during sex."

Brandon shot him a look as the tension flickered between them again. But almost immediately, he let out a reluctant laugh. "You really are an asshole, you know that?"

They both laughed again, and this time it felt almost normal.

In the hospital, Linda had slept for nearly 28 hours. Not moving. Not making a sound.

The nurses on duty had no idea that her eyes had opened. Awakened from her sleep as she sensed something nearby.

She stared at the ceiling for a beat, not knowing where she was, before looking around.

Despite the darkness, she could tell it was a hospital room, and from the ache in her body, that she had been injured. She quickly remembered what had happened to her in the bedroom.

In a panic, she sat up and checked herself over. Noticing the IV needle in her arm, she yanked it out with a yelp. She had to find out what was happening. Something wasn't right. She could feel it in every fiber of her being.

Quickly, she got out of bed and limped over to the door, peering out.

The corridor was quiet, and as she looked both ways, she could not see a soul.

Stepping out barefoot, she did not notice the drops of blood that fell from where the IV had been pulled out, and onto the cold floor.

The lights above hummed loudly, making what was a small headache more pronounced and throbbing.

She stepped slowly out, being as quiet as she could as she hobbled down the corridor. Her knee was painful to move, as was the rest of her body. She felt battered.

Reaching a corner, she hesitated for a second before peeking around it.

It was just another empty corridor running past a large, empty admitting desk.

Taking a few steps, she listened.

There was no sound of anything.

She exhaled, relieved.

She had sensed something, but all she saw was a sleeping hospital.

She turned to go back to her room and immediately jolted.

A ghostly figure stood across from her.

Her heart leapt... but as she stared, she realized it was just her own reflection in the glass of the admitting desk. Her gown. Her posture. Her own wide, fearful eyes staring back.

She laughed nervously under her breath as she turned back to her room.

There he was.

Standing in her way.

A man she had never seen before.

But Jim had.

A tall man, wearing a coat from the '30s, with a

grey beard, eyes of hatred and a wide, cruel, perverse smile.

In his hand, he held a large axe.

Baring his teeth, he raised the weapon and rushed toward her.

The blade swung through the air.

For a fleeting moment, Linda felt a coldness across her neck...

...then her world began to tilt.

Her vision spun, the corridor flipped over and over in her eyes.

The impact on the floor jarred the top of her skull, and as she stared forward, unable to blink. She could see, there in front of her... was her own body. Standing there, headless, staggering. Before her knees gave way and the body crumpled to the floor.

Linda woke up screaming, fists clenched into the hospital sheets, her whole body soaked with sweat, seeping through her hospital gown.

Her screams continued as she remembered her own decapitation with crystal clarity.

Down the corridor, at the admitting desk, two nurses dropped what they were doing and ran toward the screaming patient.

Above the entrance to the narrow shop, a wooden hand-carved sign hung that said *Wanda's Witchcraft*

Warehouse. Inside was an incense-soaked emporium where shelves bent under heavy, old books, and a large display by the cash register offered all kinds of magic crystals for sale.

The bell on the door chimed as Brandon walked out, carrying a large paper bag under his arm.

On the street, Jim was resting on the hood of the car.

He stood up as Brandon approached.

"You get it?" he asked.

Brandon reached into the bag and pulled out a brand-new Ouija board.

Jim smiled, then his expression fell. "Brandon, can't this all be bullshit please? I really hate that we are gonna do this."

"Well, we need it to contact David. Only option we have. Otherwise, we just go back empty handed, with our dicks tucked between our legs."

Jim stared down at it with disdain. "God," he said. "This whole mess bites the big one."

The wooden dock had been deserted and forgotten for many years. No boats were moored here anymore, as they used to be, and the jetty still lay in splintered ruins, untouched for thirty years.

The nearby boathouse was left in a similar state of abandonment. A rotten wooden frame with none of its windows unbroken, it was decrepit.

Brandon and Jim sat cross-legged, facing each other

between the lakeshore and the boathouse. Beside them stood a tall stack of heavy old crates, secured to the building with rope.

The Ouija board lay on the ground between them. Jim watched in silence as Brandon took the planchette and placed it at the center.

"I thought it had to be on our knees," Jim asked. "You know, all that connection stuff you said at the party."

Brandon didn't look up. "No, not this time. Since this is the place he died, contact with his spirit should be strong. No need to use our own energy to reach out. Think of bodies like a radio booster, you don't need one if the signal comes from here."

Jim looked a bit worried. "Not *too* strong, I hope."

Brandon smiled, trying to sell something he had no real idea about. He did not know if what he was saying was true. He was guessing it all, but he had to believe it was all as he said, or he might run and never look back. "Don't worry. If I'm right about Linda being his portal, he won't be able to manifest physically here, he only can near her. Here, he should just be able to talk."

"And what if you're wrong? What if the Ouija's *still* his portal? We're gonna be opening the door if we use this. Opening it up enough for him to get us like he got the others."

"I'm *not* wrong, I can't be.... I..." Brandon said, trying to convince himself as much as Jim. "Look, all we know is best guess anyway. No one knows every-thing about this. Let's say he can get through and hurt us here. Well, at least he isn't with Linda. But Linda *has* to be his portal. It's the only thing that makes any sense."

"Give me a percentage about how much you believe what you just said?"

Brandon smiled, not wanting to answer. "Just don't speak, okay? We don't want to piss anyone off. Besides, David can't do anything while Linda's unconscious, right?"

At the hospital's discharge desk, Linda stood in her own clothes, ready to check herself out. Across the counter, a nurse handed her a pen to sign her release forms. But before she could put pen to paper, Dr. Morton walked over.

"Ms. Brewster, I've just been told that you are signing out against medical advice? We really need to run a few more tests. We just—"

"No, I'm fine," Linda cut in, as she smiled at the doctor. "I just want to go home, okay? No more tests. No more poking and prodding. I'll get my own answers." She turned back and signed the form without waiting any longer.

Morton was powerless to stop her as Linda smiled and left.

Their fingers gently touched the edge of the planchette as it moved in a figure-eight pattern across the board.

Jim stared in surprise. He had seen other people use a Ouija before, and been naturally cynical about it, yet had never used one himself. Even now, as the planchette moved of its own accord, he still had a tough time believing in ghosts. But he could not deny that there was some power at work, and that his beliefs meant nothing to the facts.

Brandon spoke in a calm and even tone. "David, do you know me?"

The planchette glided slowly to YES.

"Do you know why we're here?"

YES.

Brandon looked at Jim, worried about the next question, before having the nerve to say it. "Please, David... Please tell me, and don't just run away. Why are you terrorizing Linda?"

The planchette moved.

N.

O.

"No? No what?" Brandon asked. "What do you mean?"

The planchette lingered before sliding across to the T.

"N-O-T," Jim whispered. "Not terrorizing?"

Brandon nodded, trying to understand. "David... are you saying you're not the one doing this to Linda?" The planchette moved back to YES.

Jim raised an eyebrow. "Then who the hell is?" he asked loudly.

Brandon looked up nervously. "Shhh," he whispered. "We can't scare him off."

But Jim's question was answered anyway.

Neither of them expected the speed the planchette spelled the next word.

E.

V.

I.

L.

The planchette quickly resumed its figure eight pattern.

"Evil?" Jim said.

Both felt anxious as they sat there, until Brandon realized something.

"Wait, wait, wait." he said, leaning into the board.

"David, you *were* at Jim's party, weren't you?" The planchette slid to *YES*.

"And you flattened my tire?"

YES.

"Did you kill Lloyd at the construction site?"

NO.

"Did you kill Zarabeth?"

NO.

"But... you did speak to us through her."

NO.

It circled about before landing again and again.

NO.

NO.

NO.

NO.

"Who the hell did we talk to, Brandon?"

The planchette didn't hesitate. It answered him straight away.

E.

V.

I.

L.

"Again with the evil?!" Jim said, exasperated. "I know I'm not supposed to talk, and you've made it crystal clear you don't like me, but this is all for Linda. So can you please just answer us and ditch all the cryptic shit?"

Brandon was more level-headed in his response. "David, is this 'evil' another spirit that has come through? Pretending to be you?"

YES.

"Okay... So, tell me... Compared to you... Is it powerful? Did it make you leave?"

YES.

"I really want him to say no to this one..." Brandon said as he moved his gaze back to the board. "David... Is this spirit's name Malfeitor?"

YES.

"Who?" Jim asked.

"Zarabeth mentioned it. Didn't know what she meant, but she spoke like it was really bad." Brandon said as he suddenly thought of something.

"David? This is important. Has Linda *ever* contacted you when I wasn't there?"

The planchette moved to NO.

Jim's expression had shifted from skeptical to something colder. Something closer to fear. "David, so all that stuff where you were calling me cruel through Zarabeth, that you hated me... That wasn't you?"

NO.

"David, who is Malfeitor?" Brandon asked.

H.

E.

R.

The figure eight pattern resumed.

"Her? Who's her?" Jim asked.

Brandon shrugged. "David... do you mean Linda is Malfeitor?"

The planchette moved to *NO.*

"Then who is HER?"

The planchette started to move. Too fast to be spelling anything. It scrawled random loops across the board, in no particular pattern.

Jim stared. "What's wrong with him?"

"I don't know. He's agitated."

Their fingers barely stayed touching as the planchette moved across the board erratically. "David, please calm down... What's wrong?"

It kept moving, frenzied. They watched it spin, as Jim remembered something.

"Hey. Didn't you say they're lousy spellers?"

Brandon nodded. "David, did you misspell the word?"

The motion stopped and shifted to the word *YES.*

"All right... David... Take your time and try again. Now, please tell me... Who is Malfeitor?"

The planchette slowed, carefully inching this time.

H.

E.

R.

Then it stopped.

"What happened?" Jim asked.

Brandon tapped on the planchette lightly. "I think we lost him. It happens sometimes... David? Are you still here?"

Nothing.

"David?"

Jim's voice was quiet. "Can we get him back?"

"I don't know..."

Jim looked at the board again. "'H-E-R... What was he trying to say?"

"I don't know," Brandon said in frustration. "David?! David?!"

Jim stared down, his mouth moving like he was working it out phonetically.

"H... E... R... He.. Her... Her."

He stared at the planchette. It had moved to the next letter without either of them noticing.

It was now sitting on the letter E.

Jim's voice was a whisper now. "H.E.R.E... Here... Malfeitor is *here*?"

"He can't be," Brandon said. "That would mean—"

SNAP!

The ropes that tied the crates to the side of the boathouse broke apart and loosened all at once.

The sound was deafening as the heavy clatter of wooden crates toppled, falling onto Jim and Brandon.

Jim tried to stand but never got the chance. A wave of heavy wood knocked him to the deck and covered him.

Brandon jumped backward. He got clear of most of the debris, but not all. One of the last crates clipped his foot, and that was enough. His body tumbled backward past the edge of the boathouse and flipped him over the edge into the water.

The lake took him with ease.

One moment he was flailing against empty air, the next he was gone, sucked beneath the surface like a heavy stone.

The water splashed for a second, then fell to ripples, before Brandon managed to claw his way back to the surface.

He burst up a few yards out from shore, coughing up lake water and gasping as he spluttered. His arms flailed about as he tried to stay afloat.

His eyes soon locked on the dock. To the pile of crates that now lay in a heap on top of Jim, whose arm poked out from underneath.

"Jim?!" Brandon shouted, as he started to swim forward. He kicked hard and swallowed more water as he yelled again. "*Jim?!*"

That's when the ripple came. Not from him, not from the splashing he was causing, but from the side of the boathouse. It broke the surface a dozen yards away. Moving toward him in a clean, deliberate direction. Like a monster underneath the water about to breach.

Brandon stopped as he saw the ripple surging toward him.

Turning the other way, he yelled out in fear as he frantically turned and swam as fast as he could toward the nearby broken jetty. His feet kicked while his arms slapped at the water in terror.

But the wake followed him much faster than he could move. Easily narrowing the gap between them.

Brandon reached the jetty base and lunged for the ladder.

He reached up as far as he could. His fingers caught a rung.

He scrambled, kicking as he pulled himself halfway out of the water.

The ripple, now right behind him, reached his shoes and stopped.

It didn't crash upon him. Didn't leap out of the water to drag him back down. It just slowed as it got to him, then in total silence, melted back into the lake like it had never been there to begin with.

Brandon remained clinging to the ladder. He could not help but laugh. A single, high breathless sound. A relieved exhalation that he was alive.

He stayed there, holding onto the rung, looking out to the lake where the wave disappeared.

That's why he didn't see it coming. He was looking the wrong way.

Something slammed into the side of his head. Something fast and violent, just a blur. A wet impact echoed off the dock as his body went limp.

Blood hit the remains of the jetty in a thick spray.

Nothing moved except the rise and fall of broken crates stacked beside the boathouse, shifting slightly as Jim stirred beneath the debris. A groan escaped him, followed by the creak of wood as he struggled to move under the weight that had fallen on him. As he forced himself to sit up, pushing the large amount of wood off, his hand instinctively reached for the sharp pain on his face. His fingers touched crusted blood, dried around a deep gash now across his cheekbone.

He moved slowly and unsteadily, pushing the last of the crates off him. He sat up with a grunt, as his whole body ached.

"Brandon," he croaked, before repeating, louder. "Brandon?"

The only sound that replied was the dull slap of waves against the water's edge.

Jim dragged himself to his feet, one arm wrapped around his ribs, and took a wheezing breath in. He limped over and looked around the waterline. He winced as he walked down to the shore, each movement sending a fresh wave of agony through him.

Kneeling at the lake's edge, he reached down and splashed his face with water, trying to rinse the blood, and clean the wound as best as he could.

His hands were shaking, and as the water hit, he could not help but cry out with pain.

The lake seemed quiet and calm.

He knew that Brandon must be here somewhere but found himself staring at himself in the water.

Reflections were never forgiving; they were the truth, unfiltered, unvarnished, and, more often than not, unwelcome. That had always been in Jim's opinion. To him, the reflection was more than a mere optical phenomenon, it was a judgment. An unyielding mirror of the reality that faced it. Whether it was in the sheen of polished glass, the ripples of water, or the accusatory gleam of someone else's eyes, reflections were the truest of lenses. They revealed everything, the beauty, the flaws, the cracks beneath the surfaces. And now, as he stared down at himself, Jim saw only one thing. Failure.

Failure with Brandon. Allowing and even encouraging their friendship to fail.

Failure with Susan. Not seeing his actions pushed her so far.

Failure with Lloyd. Unable to save him from a horrific death.

Failure with Zarabeth. He had been rude to her, despite not knowing her, and that might have been one of her final experiences.

Failure with his own mind. He mocked and ridiculed every part of this spirit talk. The Ouija board. Why? Because he was arrogant. He hated that he was.

And mostly, he felt a failure with Linda. The reflection didn't lie.

As he dwelt in his morose thoughts, he did not notice the ripples in the water.

He was too locked in his thoughts to stop the hand that shot up from the depths of the water, followed by the horrific moan that breached the surface.

Fingers latched onto Jim's collar before he could even register what was happening. The grip was ice-cold and rigid, clamping down on him as he stumbled backward, dragging the weight with him.

"Brandon!" he cried out, realizing who it was.

Pulled down onto the shore, Jim rolled his friend over. "Brandon, what happened?" he said, terrified.

But what was left of Brandon's face barely resembled a person.

"No," Jim began to sob.

Brandon's skin was shredded. Slashed and deeply torn. His eyes had been hacked out, like the rest of his features. There was no mouth. No nose. No cheeks nor brow. His whole head was now just a pit of bone and bloody pulp.

Jim's hands hovered over the gore, as he shook uncontrollably.

"Please... No," he cried.

He could stop himself from holding the side of his friend's ruined face.

Sitting there at the water's edge, a deep, hoarse cry of anguish tore out of Jim. Full of things that had waited too long to escape. Years of hurt, frustration and guilt. He could not even try to stop it. It just tore through his throat and out across the lake.

Chapter Eight

The dumpster sat outside the Lakewood Apartments, having not been emptied for the past few days. As the evening started to come in, the shadows began to grow, coating the neighborhood.

Linda had come back from the hospital, walked across the lawn and peered into the dumpster. There, lying on top of the household waste was the Ouija board. Undamaged, open, facing up at her. She stared at it, pondering what she should do. But any doubt she had seemed to disappear when she touched its edges.

She didn't even consider why she had walked over here from the taxi. To the dumpster of all things. She didn't know why she hadn't just walked straight inside. She had no idea that Jim had even thrown the board down there. Yet, as she got out of her ride, she had walked over the lawn, straight to the exact place the board had been discarded.

She did not consider how or why, as now, as she held the board close to her chest, it filled her with a sense of calm—a calm that dulled her thoughts. She then picked up the planchette that sat nestled in the grass beneath her, again having no idea it was even there before she grabbed it.

As she slowly climbed the staircase, the board was immovably held in her grasp. With a distant look, her expression was lost and unreadable. There was no urgency. No fear. No emotion.

Inside the apartment, the living room was dark.

Earlier that day, the door to the bedroom that Jim had broken to save her had been replaced. She didn't even notice it, nor even consider the memory; the whole event seemed blurred now, like it belonged to someone else.

Flicking on a lamp, she walked straight over to the couch and sat down in the muted orange glow.

Resting the board on her knees, she placed the planchette on top.

For a minute, she sat still, staring at the letters, now feeling a fear within her, but a fear that could not stop her using the board.

Her fingers hesitated, then rested gently upon the edge of the planchette.

"David?" she asked quietly. "David, are you here?" Silence pressed in around her.

The planchette didn't move.

Linda cleared her throat and tried again.

"David, please answer me... Where's Jim?" Her

whole body was filled with dread. "Has something happened? Tell me, please?" Still nothing.

"Answer me, dammit!"

Again, the planchette didn't twitch. Didn't so much as tremble.

Standing up sharply, with teeth gritted, she slammed the board onto the coffee table.

"Fuck you, you bastard," she shouted.

But then the realization sank in. She had picked up the board, knowing where it was. It wanted her to pick it up. It made her.

"What the fuck do you want from me?" she added, screaming more to the apartment around her than the board itself.

Nothing and no one answered. The home felt empty.

"God damnit," she whispered to herself. "Get a grip, Linda."

Jim *must* have told her that he threw the board away when he brought her to the hospital. Before she lost consciousness. Her mind was a mess, she *must* have been told, but somehow forgot... *Right?*

As she tried to impose logic on an illogical situation, a flicker of amusement crossed her face, almost a smile, at the sheer absurdity of having expected anything different. She sneered at the board, then turned and walked into the bedroom, stripping off her clothes one by one, letting them drop where they fell.

. . .

The bathroom mirror was fogged by the time the shower had started to run hot. Linda was still shaking off her negative thoughts as she stepped under the steam.

Jim and Brandon were fine. Jim left her that note in the hospital. They are together... miraculously. The worst thing that could happen is that they would strangle each other.

She was fine.

David was gone.

All would be back to normal soon.

The ropes that had once held the crates to the boathouse now swung freely in the nighttime breeze. Their ends were sliced in straight lines. There was no fraying, nor torn fibers. All had been cut. Clean and intentional.

A large, steady, gloved hand reached out and took one of the cut ropes, turning it over in his grip. Sergeant Allen examined it closely.

Jim was beside him, his cheek now wrapped in a bandage, looking drained of everything, his eyes were bloodshot from the emotional strain.

"The ropes were cut," Allen said. "You still claiming that they just broke on you?"

"I have no idea what happened," Jim sighed. "All I know is that I heard them all snap real damn loud, and then all the crates fell on me."

"And they knocked you out?" The Sergeant spoke

in a tone that clearly stated that he did not believe a word that was being said.

Jim tried to hide his frustration, but he couldn't keep it from showing. "Exactly, and I've got the damn bruises and cuts to prove it."

"And when you came to, Mr. Morar... your friend was dead?"

Jim could only nod, as the sight of Brandon's massacred face shone clearly in his mind. Facing him in its horrific glory.

Allen regarded Jim with the same slow patience he used with anyone he considered to be lying. "And just so I have it straight... The two of you drove all the way from Fairfield, *just* to visit this part of the lake?"

"Yes, I told you...!" Jim's voice whined. "Please, Lieutenant—"

"*Sergeant*," Allen corrected him.

"Sorry... Sergeant ..." Jim muttered. "We've been over this a hundred times. Look, my friend... he's dead—"

The sentence stopped halfway through.

The word had weight to it now. Dead.

Brandon was dead. Like Lloyd and Susan.

He turned to one side, where two officers were loading the body bag into the back of a van, as the coroner stood by watching. The bag sagged at the top, where Brandon's head had been.

The Sergeant studied Jim's face and saw the genuine hurt.

He had spent his whole career being surprised at

what people were capable of. So much so that it made him numb to most emotions. People lie. People deceive. People are cruel. But this made him cold, and he knew that. From seeing the genuine emotion in Jim's face, Allen forced himself to think that maybe his assumption was wrong. Maybe this was not as it seemed, and that this kid was telling the truth.

The edge in Allen's voice softened a little as he spoke. "All right," he said. "Why don't you go back to your motel? We'll call you tomorrow."

"Sergeant Allen." The coroner shouted over from the back of the van.

Allen raised a hand to wave him off and turned back to Jim. "Don't leave the city, and don't go back to Fairfield until we speak, understand?"

Jim nodded. He didn't know what else to do. He walked slowly to Brandon's car parked at the edge of the dock. His posture was sagging. There was no more argument, fight or attitude left in him. He felt empty.

He could hear Brandon now, up on his cloud, screaming down at him for getting in his car and turning the engine on.

The car stood still for a moment, as Jim sat in the driver's seat and took a breath in. He could still smell Brandon's aftershave.

Allen watched the car drive away, as he walked over to the back of the coroner's van.

"What've you got?" he asked.

The coroner shrugged. "Won't know for sure until

I get him back to the lab... but no way falling crates did this."

"Then what did?"

"I don't know." The coroner lowered his voice. "But whatever it was, it was sharp. And very heavy. This was an attack. And a vicious one at that."

"Damn." Allen grumbled as he turned to call across the shore, "Hawkins! Get a unit over to the 480 Motel. Tell 'em to keep an eye on Morar, but don't approach him. Just make sure he stays put."

The uniformed officer nodded and moved off toward his patrol car.

From the far side of the jetty, another voice called out. Detective Vicente. One of the plainclothes investigators on the scene. "Sergeant Allen, over here!"

Allen walked over and climbed down the ladder, onto the broken jetty and made his way around the cracked boards to where Vincente waited.

"What've you got?"

Vicente didn't answer. Just moved aside and pointed down.

From under a fallen piece of debris. He had found something.

An axe-hammer. Resting quietly among the splintered wood. The handle was marked. Letters were carved deep enough to be seen. J.M.

Allen stared at it.

He didn't speak for several seconds, then he exhaled heavily through his nose. "Shit,' he grimaced. "That guy was so dumb as to monogram the damn murder weapon?" He cursed himself for feeling sorry for Jim, and for doubting his own intuition. "You'd better contact Fairfield P.D.," he said to Vicente. "I got a feeling that Mr. Morar will not be going back to his motel."

"Think he's heading home?"

"If he's sane..." Allen said, looking out over the lake. "He's probably heading the opposite way... but I got a feeling that kid is far from sane."

Vicente nodded in agreement.

The coroner had joined Allen by the axe-hammer. He looked down at it, then up at the sergeant. "You don't really think he would have called us if he'd done this, do you? Leaving the weapon here with his initials, okay?"

"Maybe. Maybe not. I've seen crazier. But one thing I *do* know for a fact, and something I'll bet you dimes to donuts on, is that our James Morar knows more than he's telling us."

Wanda's Witchcraft Warehouse was dark, though the sign flickered in purple neon that buzzed so loudly that anyone passing could hear it.

Jim pulled Brandon's sports car up to the curb and killed the engine.

He looked through the windshield at the store. Its windows were opaque with posters: tarot readings, spiritual cleansings, and palmistry, all next to a large sign he remembered seeing earlier: *Open for emergencies 24/7 – CALL FIRST.*

He had done just that. The number had been on

the paper bag the Ouija board had been purchased in. The one he found on the shoreline as he waited for the police to arrive.

After leaving the lake, he had driven straight to a phone box and called the number. He'd been told to wait a couple of hours, which he did by driving around aimlessly. Now he was here.

He got out, slammed the door, and rushed across the sidewalk, vanishing into the doorway without looking back.

Inside, the sickly smell of incense hit Jim hard.

"Hello? It's Jim Morar?" he called out. "I called earlier?"

From deeper in the shop, a woman's voice floated up to him like the smoke from all the candles around.

"Okay... I think I've found it."

She emerged between two tall rows of books, hips swaying to a song only she heard. She carried with her a heavy, cloth-bound book and a look in her eye that bordered on ecstatic.

This was Wanda. This was her shop and also her world.

Her whole image was carefully crafted for effect, with a black dress that clung tightly, and a neckline deep enough to suggest a lot less than it showed. She looked like a witch, spoke like a sailor, and thought like a scientist. She was a force to be reckoned with. She flipped through the book with her long-manicured nails before looking up at Jim with a smile.

"So," she began, stopping behind the shop's counter, "I can tell you without any doubt that he's not one of your more popular cult deviants."

Jim's eyes were red, his bruises stinging. His wounds real as well as emotional. The day and night had already done their damage.

"I didn't know there were any," he replied.

"Any what?"

"Uh... *Popular* deviants."

Wanda grinned. "Oh sure. The more deviant, the better I say."

Her gaze dragged slowly down his body and back up again, totally unashamed. Like a spider sizing up a fly.

Jim was oblivious to any of it.

"What about Malfeitor?" he asked.

"Oh, I found out some stuff..." Wanda paused, as she leaned on the counter, chin propped on one hand. "But first, there is the small matter of my consultation fee. Can't give you gold without getting gold after all. With after-hours research as well, that's fifty bucks. Payable now."

Without a word, Jim reached into his pocket and brought out a small fold of money. Taking fifty dollars from the pile, he handed it over with a thin smile.

"Perfect." She took the money and tucked it into her cleavage, then turned the book around on the counter for him to see. "I think it's Carlos Malfeitor you're thinking of. He was originally from Brazil but moved to California and formed a small cult in the late twenties. *Heavily* into the occult. Human sacrifices, and so much more... His whole thing was torment. His name pops up in most books about that era, and in some of the later spirit books. That name appears nowhere else in my books. Only with him. And this book has it all. Thirty-nine, ninety-five."

She moved closer. Closer than necessary. Their faces were inches apart now, close enough for breath and for misread signals. Not that she was misreading anything.

He still had no idea, though.

"So," she said, smiling again, "are you interested?"

"Interested?"

"In buying this book."

"Oh... I don't know."

Wanda's smile didn't falter. "I'm sure I've got something here you'd like. If you're really interested in ol' Carlos, why don't you try old police files? We got loads. He will definitely be in there."

"So, he was just a Cult leader?

"Oh, no. He was way worse than that. He was a fairly notorious mass murderer back then. Killed nine people they know of, suspected dozens more. Stalked them, tormented them, basically drove them mad before chopping them up with an axe."

"Is there a picture of him?"

Wanda reached across and turned the page.

There he was.

Jim did not expect to see *that* man. He had totally forgotten about his vision. He had forgotten the cruel looking man who held an axe. Those sharp eyes. That gray beard.

The photograph itself was a sepia tone portrait of Carlos Malfeitor looking sternly into the camera, wearing a pristine black suit.

"I've seen him before," he said, not realizing that he had just spoken out loud. "Do you know what happened to him?"

Wanda reached forward and flipped another page. "The police caught up to him around 1931... shot him down dead in his own home." She tapped the page. "Right here."

It was a photo. Grainy and yellowed, taken from above of an old Victorian house. The caption below stated the address of the residence.

In Fairfield.

On his road.

In his building.

The Lakewood Apartments.

Jim's mouth dropped open slightly.

Without a word, he ran. Out the door, gone before Wanda had the chance to say anything else.

She stood, one eyebrow raised. Slowly, she moved her gaze down to the book, shrugging off another lost customer.

. . .

The water stopped falling as Linda turned the shower knob.

It had been scalding, almost unbearable, but she'd welcomed the sting, even forced it. She needed the distraction. She needed something to cut through the chaos. The world felt like it was spinning faster and faster, out of control, but the boiling heat was something she could choose. She'd made the water too hot on purpose.

Now in the cubicle, her skin felt raw, but alive. It was only a small victory, but one she was glad about.

She pushed at the shower door, ready to dry off and try to get some sleep. Not that she thought that she would be able to relax.

The door didn't budge.

She tried again. Pushing at it harder this time.

Before she could try a third time, the knob under the shower head gave a squeak as it turned on its own.

From the head came the water.

Not hot like before but boiling.

It hit her shoulder and side first, then her face.

She screamed and recoiled against the tiled wall. Her fingers clawing for the knob, having to reach through the jet of boiling water.

She screamed wildly from the pain and twisted the knob hard. But it did not stop the water, it just came off in her hand.

Steam filled the cubicle within seconds, billowing out, suffocating, as it hit her lungs painfully.

She could only scream more as she dropped it to

the floor and tried to back away. But there was no escape. The water kept on coming. Hotter and hotter.

She backed against the tile, gasping. Panic rose behind her ribs and pounded in her throat.

She saw the towel, draped across the top of the shower door.

She snatched it, wound it tightly around her fist, and, without a second thought, drove it hard into the glass.

The pane shattered, shards bursting outward as her covered fist punched through. With a surge of power, she hurled her body forward, crashing through the broken frame. Jagged shards sliced into her skin as she pushed herself through. Her burning skin did not feel the pain the glass caused, as a dozen long, deep cuts over her body formed, leaking large streams of blood.

As her foot hit the tile, into a mixture of blood and water, she slipped. She managed to catch herself against the sink with both hands, as her chest painfully heaved. Then the pain from the glass cuts began to be felt.

For a second, everything was agony. The sound of the water behind her hissed like someone laughing.

She didn't cry, though. Not this time. Her screams were angry as well as hurt.

She grabbed another towel off the rail and wrapped it around herself, barely covering the burns and bleeding wounds.

Staggering through the bedroom, her path was

immediately cut off as the door to the living room slammed shut. No wind, no warning.

She yanked at the handle with both hands.

It did not open. It did not move or even rattle. It felt fused to the frame. Sealed from the other side.

She pulled harder, but like the shower door, it was useless. She would only get out by smashing her way through. But this was not glass or something she could easily punch her way out of.

Terrified, she looked back into the room, knowing that someone had to have been in there with her. She moved back until her shoulders pressed against the door. The towel clung to her damp and bloody skin, getting more soaked by the second.

With her wound bleeding through the towel, her breathing shallow, she started to feel dizzier and dizzier.

The phone booth was cracked and graffiti covered, tucked to one side of a closed gas station. Jim stood inside, worried. Phone in one hand.

He waited as the line rang.

'*How can I direct your call?*' the hospital switchboard operator said in a bored tone.

"I'd like to speak to Linda Brewster," he said with urgency. "She's a patient in room 310." He paused for a second before correcting himself. "No, she's in 375! It's an emergency!"

'One second, please.' The voice said, before the line switched to some banal holding music.

The call soon clicked back on.

'*We had a Ms. Linda Brewster, but she checked herself out. May I ask who you are?*'

"What? When?"

'*I'm sorry, who is this?*'

He didn't wait to explain. He slammed the receiver down and bolted from the booth.

Linda's white-knuckled hand was again trying to open the door.

Through her dizziness, her hands grabbed the handle. She twisted, pulled, even braced a foot against the wall, but the door didn't give. It was unmoving.

She let go, gasping, keeping an eye on the room behind her. She felt weaker and weaker with each passing moment. The bleeding had stopped, but she had lost enough blood that it was affecting her. And with the blood loss, as her burned skin started to cool, she began to shiver uncontrollably. She dropped the bloody damp towel, rushed forward and grabbed the bathrobe lying on the bed.

As she tied the belt tight, something caught her eye. Something on the bed. Something that the robe had covered until now.

There was the Ouija board.

She hadn't brought it into the room. She hadn't even touched it since slamming it onto the coffee table.

But it was here, lying square in the middle of the bed.

A low sound started to emanate from a corner next to the bed, catching her fearful attention. She backed away as she saw the shape of the shadows changing. Undulating. As if something was in it. She couldn't see what it was but could tell that it was something.

Then the shadow rushed toward her at incredible speed.

Linda screamed.

The highway passed in a long blur.

The sports car was driven into a wail that bordered on screaming, as its headlights brightly lit the way.

Inside, Jim's hands gripped the wheel tight. He had not gone back to the motel and was now ignoring all that the sergeant had told him. He knew that this would make him more of a suspect, but he had no choice. He could not try to explain this to anyone. He had to do this himself. He had to get to Linda.

The road at this hour was deserted, and when the car went roaring by, it soon disappeared into the night, taking all the sounds along with it.

The front door slammed open hard enough to be heard from outside.

Jim ran into the apartment, out of breath, but stopped dead in his tracks after a single step.

The entire apartment had been destroyed.

The couch was hacked apart down the middle, its cushions torn and splayed open. Picture frames had been shattered; their glass scattered over the floor. The walls were littered with hacked gashes across almost every part of the plasterwork. The television had been smashed. All electric cords severed. This wasn't the result of a struggle, it was pure destruction.

Jim took a step forward, surveying with an all-encompassing worry.

And there it was, on the coffee table.

The Ouija board.

It lay perfectly intact, eerily untouched amid the wreckage. The planchette resting on its surface expectantly.

Jim approached the table, his head shaking involuntarily as he stared down at the board. He couldn't take his eyes off it. He had thrown it away, and now it was back, looking in as perfect a condition as the day it had been made. Better than it was before.

Then came a shriek from behind him.

He whirled and caught sight of Linda as she ran toward him, face wild in fury, gripping the fire axe from the glass case in the lobby in both hands, raised about her head.

She screamed maniacally as she swung. The axe came down in a violent arc.

Jim launched himself sideways as the blade buried itself into the bookcase behind him, cracking through its top shelf and into the books.

Linda grimaced as she followed his every step, every movement. Her face was twisted as her eyes seethed with a fury he did not recognize. She growled and held the axe high again, ready to attack.

Like a marionette, her body moved in jolted bursts. Her steps seemed like a struggle. As she stared at Jim with murderous intent, her mouth hung open, and drool seeped out.

They circled each other around the living room, locked in an orbit. Moving slowly, tensely, their eyes fixed unflinchingly on each other.

Jim's hands raised cautiously.

"Linda... please. No..." he said. "I'm trying to help you."

Her smile twisted into a grimace.

The voice that came out of her mouth was deep and ugly, scraped from the inside of her throat. A grotesque parody of what she would usually sound like.

"How are you enjoying it?" she leered. "I'm having so much fun seeing your mind break."

"Please, Linda," he said, staring at her fearfully. "I just want to help you."

"You want to help me?" she giggled. "Fine. Then stop moving."

Jim glanced toward the apartment door that he had left open.

Linda grinned as he made a break to escape.

Before he could get close, the door slammed shut.

He spun back, just in time to see the axe coming at him again.

It hit the doorframe, narrowly missing his skull, slicing through the air and embedding itself in the wood.

Jim lunged, grabbed her by the shoulders, and shoved her forward. The axe stayed stuck in the frame, as they fell back into the living room, crashing over the coffee table. Knocking the Ouija board to the floor.

The table splintered into pieces under their weight, in a mess of limbs and screaming.

Without missing a beat, Linda clambered on top of Jim, straddling him as she wrapped her hands around his neck.

As she squeezed, her fingers felt beyond cold and were impossibly strong.

Jim tried to breathe as the air was being suffocated from him. In vain, he clawed desperately at her wrists, but as he did, his vision started to blur.

She moved closer to his face as she choked the life from him. Grinning, the drool tipped from her lips and down onto his gasping face.

With all his might, he could only do one thing: strike at her with his fists. But his strength was low and his punches into her did nothing. She didn't flinch or move to the impact.

"That was cute," she laughed.

He tried to hit her again with everything he had. But his arms had little space to swing. She rested like dead weight upon him, draining his life away with her grasp.

His hands clawed at the floor, groping blindly, not knowing what he could do.

His fingers closed around something metal.

A letter opener.

He gripped it tightly then moved the point up to her ribs. Pressing it into her.

Linda stopped choking him the moment she felt the blade against her. Her grip loosened, though her hands didn't move.

She peered down, then back at him. Her smile grew wider.

"Go ahead, James," she said, with a guttural glee. "What are you waiting for? Kill your precious Linda if you must."

Jim's eyes widened as it all became very clear. He'd no time to think when he was being attacked before. He had rushed in here not knowing what to expect, but when he saw her attack, he could not process what was happening. But looking up at her, at the expression on her face that ached for murder, he knew this was not her.

Progressive entrapment.

Possession.

Jim understood whose eyes he was now looking up at.

Her grip around his throat started to tighten once more.

This wasn't Linda. It was him. "Carlos Malfeitor," he gasped.

To which the grip just got tighter, and Linda's grin got toothier.

"At your service," she said with a look.

"Linda," Jim choked out. "Please. Fight him. You've got to fight him." He coughed in a wheeze as he tried to breathe. "I... I love you."

Immediately, something changed.

Her grip loosened. Her face softened. The distortion in her voice slipped away, replaced by a more fragile tone.

"Jim?" she said. Sounding like herself once more, sitting back. Looking terrified.

He inhaled sharply, trying to regain his breathing. He began to sit as he spoke, looking relieved. "Linda... thank God, I—"

But she slammed him back down.

The grin was back. The voice was wrong once more.

"Not that easy, James," she said with glee. "Not... that... easy."

Her hands clamped around his throat once more. Crushing his windpipe as her grip tightened. She had been holding back before, but now she was using all her possessed strength. The bones in his neck cracked under pressure as she squeezed tighter and tighter. And as she did, his vision started to fade, his lips had started to turn blue, as his lungs constricted in agony.

Just before the light vanished out of him entirely,

he gripped harder on the letter opener still in his hands and thrust its blade deep into her hip.

She wailed like an animal in pain, grasping at the wound as she collapsed to one side.

Jim, barely holding onto his consciousness, rolled away, coughing, dragging in air as much and as fast as he could.

Climbing onto the side of the couch, he staggered to his feet—

"Don't move, asshole!" He turned around.

Jim had not heard the door open, nor the murmurs of the people standing there.

Lieutenant Dewhurst stood with his gun raised, flanked by Mrs. Moses. Both frozen in wide-eyed stare.

Dewhurst didn't lower his weapon. "Mrs. Moses, please go downstairs and call for backup. Tell them Lieutenant Dewhurst needs a black and white and a couple of uniforms, okay? Can you remember that?"

Mrs. Moses didn't answer; she ran as fast as her legs could carry her back to her apartment. Dewhurst walked inside the apartment, kicking the door shut behind him.

Linda was collapsed on her knees, as blood streamed from the wound around the letter opener. The blade was still lodged in her flesh.

Dewhurst approached slowly, eyes moving between them. Gun locked on Jim.

"Mr. Morar," he said, "I understand you left quite a mess up in Tahoe, didn't you?"

Jim held out his hands. "Please, listen—"

"Don't," Dewhurst commanded. Refixing his aim at Jim's head. "Not a word."

He sidled over to Linda. "Ms. Brewster, can you stand?" he said as he crouched to help her up.

He did not see the perverse grin on her face as she grabbed a broken coffee table leg and swung it hard at the policeman.

The wood cracked across Dewhurst's face. He flew backward into a tall cabinet, dropping his gun and crashing into the glass and wood. The ornamental dishes inside smashed and fell to the floor in an explosion of sharp shards.

Linda rose to her feet, with the table leg still in her hand, but her movements were sluggish. The wound in her hip had slowed her down more than she'd expected.

She wasn't fast enough to get to the Lieutenant's gun that lay in the middle of the room. Jim had already reached it.

A few feet apart, they faced each other again.

She raised the table leg, her grin returning.

Jim's hands trembled as he raised the gun towards her. He cocked it with a loud click.

Through her poisonous smile, Linda let out a small chuckle as she lowered the table leg.

"You won't kill her, James," she said. "Your *love*. You don't have that in you."

Jim swallowed. The voice was correct. He knew he could not shoot to kill her. "I can shoot you in the legs, though."

Linda laughed louder. "How will that change a thing?"

"It'll buy us some time. Me and Linda."

Linda widened her eyes, mock impressed. "Oh, will it now?"

"Time enough to fight you. Time enough for her to close whatever portal you crawled out of."

She stepped forward, casual, confident. "Portal? Do you even know what you're talking about?"

Jim clenched his jaw. He was not sure of anything.

Linda pointed, as she held the table leg up with her other hand. "You don't get it. Only you can close that, James."

"Put that down," Jim shouted, taking a step back.

"You're *so* smart, and you *still* haven't figured it out?"

She laughed. "*You're* the portal, James. Not Linda." Jim's expression fell.

"*You're* the one I opened up. *You're* the one I've been terrorizing. Think about it, how could I have murdered your friends when she wasn't there? No... Linda's mine now just out of happenstance... And for as long as you live."

Jim stared at the gun, confused. Then back up to Linda. "Bullshit," he said. "You *tried* to kill me."

"Kill? No. It was all just to scare you. You've suspected it all along, but you didn't *want* to believe it." She took a step closer. "You know you were to blame... So, if you really want to save her?" She gestured toward the gun. "Well, you've got the means right there in your hands... So, go ahead, James... *You* are the portal... Close it. Give in to the fear."

Her eyes gleamed with cruelty.

Jim stared at the pistol, as it was still aimed at her.

"But I know you won't do it," she continued. "You can't. But let us be truthful about it. You don't love her, anyway. Not that much. You loved someone else once. But Linda? No." Her smile faded as she watched him with a fake concern. "I suppose the only one you would have pulled that trigger for was Brandon, right? Isn't that why Susan *really* killed herself?" Leaning closer, she whispered playfully. "Linda knows that by the way."

Jim couldn't process any of it, as he started to cry, and his thoughts collided in a mass of confusion.

Across the room, Dewhurst stirred. He rolled onto one side, dazed, blinking the blood from one eye as it poured down from a wound on his brow.

Linda lowered the table leg, still facing Jim. "And if you pull the trigger, sure it will save Linda... but she doesn't control a thing. You will just sever a link. That's all. Is *that* worth it? Just for her, who you pretend to love? Instead, I'll just remain stuck to you. So, you have a choice... let her kill you, or you kill her. Either way is good for me. As long as there is chaos. As long as there is cruelty... as long as someone dies." The glee on her face was terrifying.

Jim hesitated as a tear fell down his cheek.

She continued. "Or I may be lying about it all. I

may be playing with you to see what you will do...So pick a path... Who will you kill to destroy me? Her or you? Take a chance. It's 50/50. Split odds. "

Jim couldn't think straight. Was all that she said right? Was he to blame for everything? Was he the portal? Was all of this started because of him? Would killing himself solve it? Would killing her?

Not knowing what else to do, he firmly gripped the gun and turned it to his own head, pressing it hard against his temple.

Jim closed his eyes.

"I love you Linda," he sobbed. "I do... No matter what happened before... I love you so much... I just was too scared to say it to you, because I don't deserve you."

Linda's expression faltered as something twisted inside her.

Jim cried out as he started to put pressure on the trigger.

In an instant, Linda... the real Linda... clawed back into her own mind for a second.

"Jim, no!" she screamed. "He's lying!"

Jim's eyes opened, and he let the gun drop to his side, pulled back into the moment by her voice. In front of him, on the floor, something caught his attention. Without knowing what else to do, he raised the gun again and aimed it at the remains of the coffee table, and the Ouija board lying among its splintered wood.

He pulled the trigger.

A shot rang out.

The bullet blasted through the middle of the board, and as it did, the monster within Linda roared in fury, thrown back against the wall as if the bullet had in fact hit it through her.

"Yes!" The real Linda shouted, as a terrifying bellow from Carlos Malfeitor took over. "NO!" He screamed through her.

Determined, Jim walked over and shot the Ouija again. A second hole blasted through it, and as it did, the whole board started to rise off the floor of its own accord. Round and round it started to spin, impossibly levitating in mid-air.

He shot a third time.

Linda screamed a twisted, monstrous cry, as her body jerked.

Jim fired again.

Another hole tore through the board as it flipped around, remaining hanging and spinning in place.

Then Jim emptied the rest of the bullets into it.

Three more shots, as fast as he could pull the trigger.

As the holes ripped through, the board began to break apart, each bullet tearing into it.

"No!" Linda screeched in pain. She clutched at her chest, as she flailed around, dropping the table leg to the floor.

Her shrieks turned into furious howls.

Dewhurst got to his feet in time to see her charge, launching herself at Jim. Arms grasping out toward him.

But the bullets in the Ouija board had taken their toll as she crumbled forward, dropping down. Collapsing in a heap.

At the same time, the board that had been floating and spinning, also fell.

"Linda!" Jim yelled, still holding the empty pistol with his trembling hands.

He took a step forward.

With one last bit of strength, Linda looked up at him and screamed with hate at him.

From a force that shot from her body, it barreled toward Jim, colliding and hurling him backward. Launching him from where he stood, straight toward the bay window.

Glass shattered. Wood broke. And he was propelled through the smashing frame and into the outside.

The world fell with him.

A rainfall of glass shards caught the moonlight. Slivers drifted down around his body as he plummeted. Straight down to the Lieutenant's car, which had been hastily parked on the lawn below.

He slammed into the vehicle's roof with dead weight.

Crumpling beneath the impact, the metal buckled instantly as the windows burst out. His limbs flailed as his body bounced off the wreckage, landing with a thud onto the lawn.

He lay there, bloodied, one arm folded beneath him, the other bent behind him. His face was turned, looking up at the sky with wide, blank eyes. Glass scattered around his body, glistening among the blades of grass, like the stars in the sky above.

Within minutes, the sirens came.

* * *

The church was full as organ music crept through the building.

The nave had been lined with dozens upon dozens of white flowers.

Most guests sat on the pews in a stiff silence, some cried quietly. Familiar faces among them. Friends, acquaintances, neighbors. All those who knew Jim or Linda were seated, waiting.

The maudlin organ quickly changed its tempo, as the Wedding March began to sound from its pipes.

All eyes turned toward the altar, where Jim and Linda kissed in front of the pulpit.

The crowd applauded, whistled, and cheered.

She wore a long white gown with a veil. A vision in satin and lace.

Everything was pristine and perfect, except for the full-length leg cast that she struggled to maneuver in.

Beside her was Jim, his morning suit perfectly pressed, managing only a small, stiff smile over a neck brace.

When Linda turned to leave, her cast tangled awkwardly in her gown, nearly sending her toppling to the floor.

The crowd burst into gentle laughter.

With a grin, Jim carefully leaned down, swept Linda up into his arms, and carried her triumphantly down the aisle.

Epilogue

The apartment was empty now. Jim and the new Mrs. Morar never returned after that night. The night Carlos Malfeitor attacked. The DA had finally released the apartment back to Mrs. Moses, remnants of police tape still dangling from the doorway.

Chris was helping her clear out what was left, as Fido, his dog, lay in the hallway outside, asleep and snoring loudly.

She had no idea what she had witnessed that night, but in the days that followed, the police had attributed the chaos to a freak gas leak, at least that's what Lieutenant Dewhurst had told her when she asked. The official word was that it was an accident. No further questions were asked. No arrests made.

She had also seen Jim Morar's name in the papers. An investigation into a death at Lake Tahoe that concluded quickly and ruled an accident. Curiously,

Lieutenant Dewhurst's name had also been mentioned as assisting the detectives.

She was too old and too tired to press the matter anymore. If the police said it was all over, she was content to let it be. She was just glad that Jim and Linda had moved, as she wanted a quiet retirement. Not nights filled with screams and shouts.

All of the furniture in the apartment had long since been removed; only the broken remnants left to be cleared.

Chris and Mrs. Moses worked in silence, filling boxes with broken pieces of wood, glass and China, then dragging them toward the door to be taken downstairs.

Mrs. Moses walked out of the bedroom, as Chris had picked up something from the remnants of the coffee table. A big grin on his face.

The Ouija board, or what was left of it.

Bullet holes riddled it. Big, round gaps that broke through the printed letters and symbols.

"Look what I found," he said.

Mrs. Moses looked over. "Oh, wow, I haven't seen one of those since I was a kid."

"I didn't know they'd been around *that* long." Chris joked.

"Oh, yeah," she laughed. "But mine was made from dinosaur hide."

"I wonder if it still works," he asked, before shrugging and dropping it into a nearby box.

He grabbed the last bits of debris from the floor and

threw them on top of the board. Among the mess was the planchette. It landed on top of the Ouija, bouncing once before coming to rest.

Chris looked down at the box and smirked. "Is there anybody there?" he asked in a mocking tone, before laughing and walking away.

For a second, the planchette remained perfectly still... then slowly, ever so slowly, it began to slide... settling precisely on the word, *YES*.

T.H.E. E.N.D.

ECHO ON PUBLICATIONS

Official Novelizations
from Echo On Publication

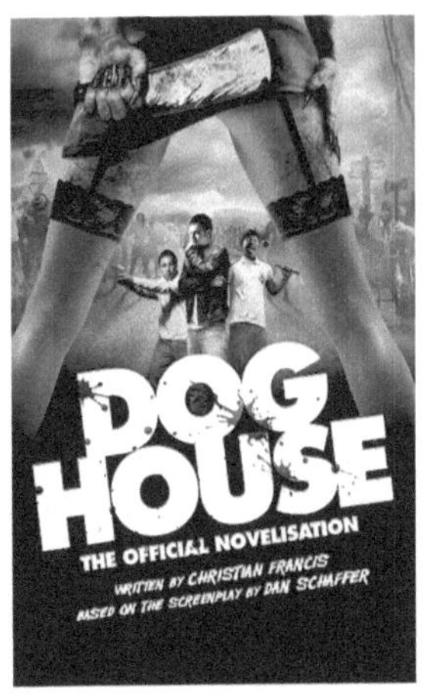

In The Mouth
of Madness

Night of The Comet

Doghouse

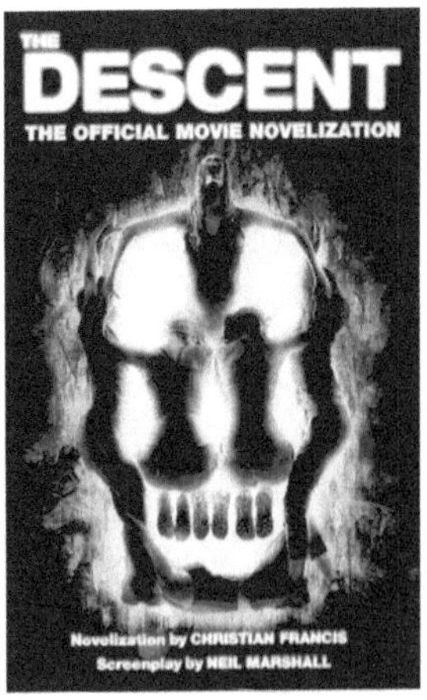

Witchboard

The Gate

The Descent
*In Partnership with
Titan Books*

check echohorror.com for more details

Official Novelizations
from Echo On Publication

Beneath Perfectiion
(Tremors)

Session 9

The First Power

Maniac Cop 1,2 & 3
*Avaialble individually or as a
collected hardcover*

Dee Snider's
Strangeland

3615 Code
Santa Claus

check echohorror.com for more details

Original Novels and Novellas
by Christian Francis

The Dead Woods
YA Horror

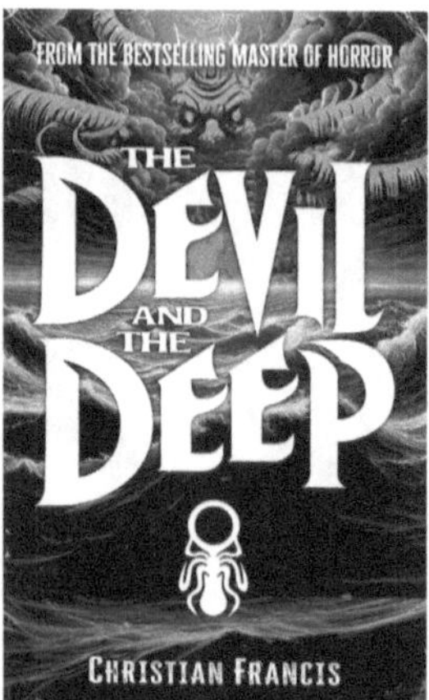

**The Devil
and The Deep**
Cosmic Horror

**The Sacrifice of
Anton Stacey**
Horror Novella

The Animus Chronicles Part 1
Everyday Monsters
Horror/Dark Fantasy

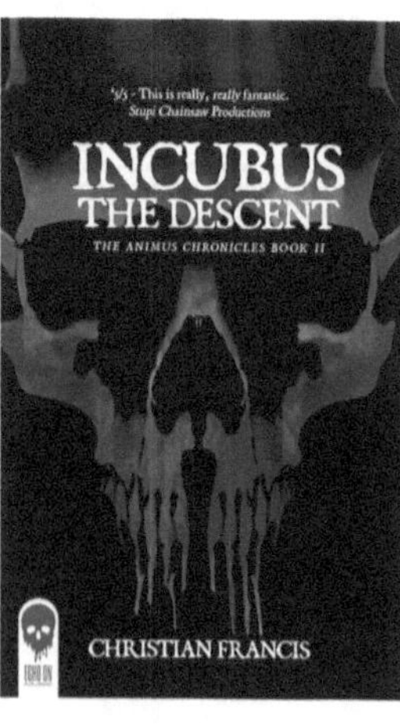

The Animus Chronicles Part 2
Incubus: The Descent
Horror/Dark Fantasy

www.ingramcontent.com/pod-product-compliance
Lightning Source LLC
Chambersburg PA
CBHW060548190726
48283CB00003B/920